BØDY

ASA NONAMI

Translated by Takami Nieda

VERTICAL.

Published by Vertical, Inc., New York

Originally published in Japanese as *Karada*
by Bungeishunju, Ltd., 2002.

ISBN 978-1-934287-37-8

Manufactured in the United States of America

First Edition

Vertical, Inc.
451 Park Avenue South, 7th Floor
New York, NY 10016
www.vertical-inc.com

Table of Contents

NAVEL

1

"You'll have to ask your father." Aiko set her coffee cup on the table and let out a small sigh.

"Oh, come on," said Minako, puffing her cheeks out to the point of bursting. "Why does it always have to be up to Dad? It's no big deal."

"That's not how it works, you know that."

"Come on!" Minako repeated, sounding thoroughly fed up. She rested an elbow on the table and looked away. "That's what you always say."

"What do you want me do? We can't very well hide it from him."

"Sure we can. This isn't plastic surgery on my face. It's my belly button. *Bell-lee buh-ton.*"

"It's still tampering with your body. I can't keep something so important from your father. How much does it cost, anyway? It must be more than twenty or thirty thousand yen."

"There's a student discount," said the teen. "It's a hundred twenty thousand."

"A hundred twenty thousand yen? That much?"

"Well, that's because the procedure isn't covered by insurance. Usually, it costs 200,000. But they offer all kinds of discounts, and for belly buttons, it's 180,000 if you're under 25 and 120,000 if you're in high school."

"A discount doctor…" muttered Aiko, reaching for a cookie.

Minako continued to pout. Then with a hand still resting against her cheek, she shifted her gaze toward Aiko. "All dad's going to say is that I don't need the procedure. He won't understand how I feel."

She's might be right, thought Aiko. But there was nothing she could do. There was a household rule that had been in place since they got married. From the beginning, her banker husband had been a busy man, growing busier with every passing year. But it was because he worked so hard that the family was promised a stable living, he would often say. He also insisted that it was up to her to look after the household and to teach the children never to take their absentee father for granted. Aiko had faithfully abided by that rule for 22 years since their arranged marriage.

Suddenly, Minako sat up straight and pleaded like a spoiled child. "*Pleease*! You understand, don't you, mom?"

"No, I don't," said Aiko with as cool an expression as she could muster.

"Why not?" Minako cried, bumping against her chair as she stood up. "Just look at this!"

The girl pulled up her lightweight sweater, revealing a pale white midriff, which Aiko had not seen in years. Nibbling on a cookie, Aiko stared at her daughter's flat stomach. How she envied her. There was a time when Aiko's stomach had looked that flat.

"It's completely round, see?"

"I think it's cute. You don't have an outie or anything."

"Hunh?" With her bare midriff still exposed, Minako twisted her body this way and that. Aiko tried to keep from laughing. Seeing her daughter, now a high school junior, posing in such a way was charming. "I can't wear a belly shirt like this!"

"That's not true. I think you'd look adorable."

"No way! You should know I had to live with this last summer, too."

With a cookie stuck in her mouth, Aiko looked first at Minako's sullen face, then her round belly button. To Aiko, the navel was proof that Minako had been connected to her inside the womb.

"The girls who show their belly buttons have thin ones. It's supposed to look like a straight line."

Now that she mentioned it, a vertical belly button might look better than a small button-shaped one, thought Aiko.

"And if you don't have that, you're just a laughingstock!" said Minako. "Are you okay with people laughing at your own daughter?"

Minako's face was the image of seriousness. Aiko nibbled on a cookie and wondered how this navel-baring fashion had become so popular. Se felt like sighing. But fads come and go. In a year or two, this obsession with belly buttons would soon be forgotten. However, Aiko knew it would be too cruel to tell a teen to wait until next year.

"Even Eri did it, you know!"

"Eri? The Saitos' daughter?"

Minako nodded. Aiko knew the girl Minako had been friends with since grade school and her mother, too. She knew Eri's mother to be a disciplinarian, serious about her child's education. There was something unapproachable about her even from the vantage point of another mother.

"I can't believe her mother agreed to it."

As Aiko sat wide-eyed in shock, Minako lowered her sweater to cover her belly button, and sat down with an air of listlessness. "She had it done secretly."

"Secretly? Eri had plastic surgery secretly?"

"It's just a belly button. Who's going to know?" said Minako, looking at her mother dead in the eye as she continued to eat a cookie. There was something fearless about the 17-year-old's look. "Still, it *is* surgery, so you need a parent's consent if you're 18 or younger."

"Well, I should think so," said Aiko. "But—you said Eri went secretly."

"She had her daddy make the call."

"Her daddy?"

"Uh-huh. Her *daddy*," said Minako, grinning meaningfully.

Washing down the bits of cookie in her mouth with coffee, Aiko leaned forward. "No..."

Minako nodded slowly. Needless to say, "daddy" referred to a male patron. She added that Eri had come up with the money for the surgery from compensated dating.

"Eri...? My goodness, I can't imagine what would happen if her mother were to find out."

"See? Some kids are like that. But here I am actually talking to you about it. Isn't that way better?"

Aiko couldn't help letting out a heavy sigh this time. Considering how other girls were secretly having plastic surgery using the money earned by prostituting themselves, she had to admit that Minako was growing up much more properly by comparison. Even so, making her hardheaded husband understand his daughter's feelings would be difficult. No doubt, he would detest the idea of Minako wearing anything that exposed her navel. Though he was rarely home, he only complained when he saw Minako on his occasional day off. *What is that hairstyle? Your eyebrows are too thin. What is a high school girl doing stinking of makeup?* It had become Aiko's role these few years to listen to his complaints after Minako stormed off sulking.

"Think about it, mom," said Minako. "Let's say I tell dad. He's just going to shoot me down like he always does, then he'll yell at you, and I'll just decide to get it done secretly, start comp dating—"

"Comp dating?"

"Compensated dating. You'd worry if that happened, wouldn't you? If I started staying out at night, hanging out with shady friends, you start finding designer clothes and bags in my room..."

"Don't you dare scare me like that."

"But that's the way Eri is now. Think of what would happen if dad ever found out about my surgery after I got to be that way."

It was true Aiko's husband often settled matters with a brusque, "You don't need it," even when the wishes of his children seemed modest enough. In fact, Aiko knew that he frequently answered this way because it was too bothersome to consider their requests properly, which was why she made a point of waiting until her husband was in a good mood and seemingly flexible to casually ask for things she truly needed. Regardless, he would never allow Minako to have plastic surgery on her navel no matter how good his mood. He was a husband who hardly understood Aiko's feelings much less his daughters'.

"Please, mom! I'll pay for half of it if I have to," said Aiko, pressing her hands together as if in prayer. "The best way to maintain a happy family and happy marriage and for me to get what I want is for you to just keep quiet about it. You already screwed up in the past. Even I will start keeping secrets from you. Is that what you want?"

Reaching for the few remaining cookies, Aiko cast an upward glance at Minako. She was talking about Chiharu. The elder daughter, a junior in college, had grown distrustful of her parents when Aiko told her husband about an upperclassman she had started dating soon after she entered college. While it was true Aiko was to blame for divulging this despite being told it was a secret, she didn't think it was anything to keep quiet about. However, her husband, who usually never took an interest in the family, checked up on her boyfriend's situation, from his financial records to even his parents' occupations and told his dreamy-eyed daughter that he was no good for her. The uproar that ensued had been the worst in the history of their marriage.

Since then, Chiharu scarcely said anything to her parents

about her private life. She took to saying, "I can't trust you," to whatever Aiko asked, and on the rare occasion her father wanted to talk, she only answered, "You wouldn't understand anyways," putting an end to further discussion. Any news about her older daughter these days came almost exclusively from Minako. As troubling as this was to Aiko, on the surface, the family remained essentially the same, and while she assumed there'd be an opportunity to mend her relationship with Chiharu, days passed into months without change.

"All right, which clinic is it?" Aiko said, finally defeated.

Minako's face lit up instantly. She dashed upstairs to her room and returned holding a teen magazine. She flipped through the pages and held out a full-page ad featuring a Caucasian model in a bikini along with the slogans:

"Summer is your chance!"

"Don't stress over it alone. Give us a call today!"

"The Arai Method is quick and painless. No hospitalization necessary. Wear makeup the next day!"

Beneath the listings for double eyelids, wrinkles, age spots, bags and liposuction, were the words, "All major credit cards and student discounts!" in a notably larger font. According to Minako, Eri had seen this ad and decided to have the surgery.

"Of course, we'll have to talk to them first," said Aiko, studying every inch of the ad.

Minako pouted again. She was the impatient type who wanted to act as soon as she made up her mind. But Aiko did not give in this time. If her high school daughter was going to have surgery, as a mother, this was more than a matter of money.

"Then when are we going? How about tomorrow? When, mom?"

After taking a long look at Minako's face, Aiko sighed quietly said, "Oh, all right" and told her daughter to fetch the phone.

2

The Arai Clinic was located inside a mixed-use building that was a 10-minute walk from Shibuya Station. When Aiko and Minako stepped out of the elevator, they were greeted by ambient sounds of chirping birds and an immaculate, brightly lit world like a day spa spread before them. The reception area was decorated with orchids and various decorative plants.

"Are you here for a consultation today?" asked the receptionist, a heavily made-up hostess-type, who looked altogether out of place for a clinic. After Aiko gave her name, the woman put on a business-like smile and pointed to the waiting area. "Please have a seat over there."

Aiko wondered whether the woman's face might be the result of repeated surgeries. Soon their name was called, and she went with Minako into the examination room, where a surprisingly young doctor greeted them with a smile. He looked to be in his mid-thirties. No, he might be even younger. Wearing a nameplate which read "Makabe" on his breast pocket, the doctor looked at Minako first and greeted her.

"You can go home right after the surgery, but you won't be able to bathe for a week. Can you do that? We'll put some gauze in there to keep pressure on it, so your belly button forms a nice depression and to keep the germs out."

They had already discussed the procedure Minako wanted to have when they made the appointment. Minako lay down on the table, and after quickly examining her navel, the doctor began to explain the procedure.

In order to sculpt the navel into a vertical depression, an incision was made to lift the skin and gather the surrounding fat and stitch it together to form a narrower navel. He made it all sound so simple. As evidence of how easy it was, Makabe explained, the procedure would take no longer than 15 or 20 minutes.

"Any adverse effects?" Aiko leaned in and asked.

"No" said Makabe, without missing a beat. "The navel is in the center of your abdomen, so it's said to be a vital part of the body, but the reality is you don't need it. It's really just a mark of your having been connected to the mother inside the womb."

"Oh," Aiko said, her eyes growing wider. She had always been told never to remove the lint out of her navel, but the doctor had essentially just told her that it was an old wives' tale.

"And besides, there isn't any muscle there, so there's no worry about muscle damage. It's a different procedure in the case of outies where there might be a perforation at the bottom, but this type of procedure really only involves retouching the surface of the body."

Minako looked happily at her mother. Aiko raised her eyebrows slightly to indicate her grudging consent.

"I think it's wonderful that you've come here with your daughter."

"Well, she is still in high school after all. I couldn't very well let her come here alone, even if she insisted on it," said Aiko as if it were totally obvious, keeping her expression as placid as possible.

Despite having a flat, stubbly face and a snobby air about him, Makabe nodded obediently. "You're absolutely right,"

"Although I understand other families aren't quite this way."

The doctor smiled. He had a pleasant face when he did. Aiko's eyes narrowed as she forced a smile. Then the doctor fixed his gaze on Aiko, his peaceful expression changing slightly. "And how about you, ma'am?"

"Me? Oh no, not my belly button, not at this age."

Dr. Makabe let out a magnanimous laugh that seemed incongruous for his age. He asked if she wanted to remove the age lines on her face.

"Jeez, mom." Minako scowled.

"If you don't mind my asking, how old are you?"

Aiko felt a little uncomfortable. What obligation did she have to answer such a young man?

"Forty-five," Minako answered instead.

Makabe nodded slowly and narrowed his eyes. "You look young for your age."

People told her so all the time. Wherever Aiko went, people remarked that she looked no older than forty or even that she looked like a friend of her daughter.

"That's too bad."

"I beg your pardon?"

"Those crow's feet—are you bothered by them at all? Maybe it has to do with your skin's condition, but they do stand out a bit."

The truth was she had noticed them. She had even tried a collagen lotion advertised on television and repeated massage treatments. The laugh lines had grown progressively more pronounced since her twenties, and now several deep lines were clearly visible around the corners of her eyes whether she was laughing or not.

"Without them, you'd probably look ten years younger. I can take care of that for you in half an hour. What do you say?"

"No, I..."

"Oh?" said the doctor in an unconcerned, candid manner. "Well, just so you know your options." Then he turned to Minako and returned to the topic of her navel surgery. Because the sutures were made of animal intestines rather than nylon, removing them would be unnecessary, he explained, and no need for a follow-up visit.

"Great!" Minako said.

Aiko wanted to ask whether some follow-up visit wasn't necessary to monitor healing after the surgery, but with the words "crow's feet" swirling inside her head she missed the chance to ask. *Ten years younger? Look like my thirties again? But none of the expensive lotions or face packs or massages work.* Aiko had come to believe that there was nothing you could do to fight age. And yet it could be easily done with a simple surgical procedure?

"So what do you think?"

Her daughters wouldn't be able to hold candle to how Aiko used to look in her younger years. She had been called beautiful, received love letters, and had more than a few suitors follow her home from school. Having grown up innocently and without hardship, Aiko had once fallen in love with an older, silver-tongued man who had charmed her into believing that he was the man of her dreams. In the end, she was thoroughly deceived and made to realize the bitterness of love.

To prevent any more unsavory types from seducing their daughter, Aiko's parents fielded offers for an arranged marriage when Aiko was still attending junior college. Though she had made a fuss of wanting to enjoy single life a while longer and to have the experience of working in an office, she ended up working only a short time before apprenticing as a wife-in-training, and eventually marrying her current husband at twenty three.

"What do you say?"

Come to think of it, no one showered her with compliments anymore. Though her husband had aggressively pursued marriage and voiced his affection for her in his own way up until their first daughter was born, after a while, he grew silent, as if he had lost interest. Aiko, too, had been so busy keeping house and raising the children that when she realized it, she had become a flabby middle-aged woman.

"Mom?"

Aiko came back to herself and found both Minako and Dr. Makabe staring at her. "Y-Yes, I see," she nodded, despite having heard nothing of what they had been talking about.

"So I'll put you down for the day after tomorrow at three p.m." Smiling, the doctor asked Minako, "Excited?"

Looking first at Makabe and then her daughter nodding emphatically, Aiko let out another sigh. Makabe turned to her with a mysterious look on his face.

"Anything the matter?" asked Makabe. "Concerns, perhaps?"

Shaking her head in a hurry, Aiko said, "To think that we live in an age of teens getting plastic surgery..."

"Yes, times are different," said Makabe with a slow, magnanimous nod. "While we continue to see rapid progress in the medical world, advances in cosmetic surgery have been especially remarkable. New techniques, of course, and anesthetics and equipment. You know, people used to say that you shouldn't tamper with the body your parents gave you. But the thinking now is if people's outlook can be a little brighter, their lives completely transformed by making a tiny change, what could be better? To an adult, the shape of your navel may not mean much, but to a teenage girl, the thought of regretting an entire summer is unbearable."

He certainly seems to have his finger on the pulse of youth, thought Aiko, rather impressed.

"A person can completely change his body how ever he pleases these days with the power of science. The point is, can that person find happiness? We here are mindful that our job is to help that person achieve the happiness they're seeking."

Happiness. Aiko was taken aback by the word. Then she imagined her face with the wrinkles gone. No doubt she *would* be happy. No longer would she be on a perpetual hunt for beauty products, no longer have to worry about how to conceal the lines every time she looked in the mirror.

"Uhm..." said Aiko at last, looking at Makabe. "By the way, how much to have the crow's feet removed?"

"Let's see." Makabe peered more enthusiastically than before to examine the corners of her eyes. "I'd say 250,000 yen just for the crow's feet."

Her brows rising only slightly, Aiko nodded slowly as if to say she was only asking.

"Well, would you at least like a consultation? During your daughter's surgery, if you'd like."

"Why not, mom?" said Minako, a mischievous grin on her face. But Aiko could only smile. The face of her husband flashed across her mind.

3

"Nine hundred thousand?" Aiko leaned forward and blinked in disbelief. The doctor before her gave a casual nod. She felt as though she'd been conned. "But the other doctor I to spoke to said 250,000."

She stuck out her lip to show that she felt dissatisfied and mistrustful. Dr. Arai looked at her and gave a small smile. The badge on his chest read "Director" in small print just below his name. At first, when she realized that the director of the clinic was consulting her himself, Aiko felt relief and a certain sense of superiority. Perhaps the younger doctor was not experienced enough when it came to facial surgery. She had felt valued as a customer. Still, hearing now that the price of something she was told would cost 250,000 yen had suddenly jumped to 900,000 yen was unacceptable.

"It's likely he only gave you an estimate for removing the crow's feet. But after taking a look myself, I can see that your entire face is beginning to sag with age, which is why these lines here are starting to come in." Dr. Arai pointed to the age lines forming along her nose and mouth, and then touched her cheeks. "And here, too. There's no tension—flabby."

Completely at the doctor's mercy, Aiko felt pathetic. Miserable, even. Though she'd been aware of these changes herself, she didn't think they would be noticeable to anyone else. Not even her husband had said anything.

"Even if we were to remove the crow's feet, there's still the overall balance of your face to consider. If we smoothed out the skin just around the eyes, it might only draw more attention to that area."

The doctor sat back in his chair and looked at her face again. His explanation made a lot of sense. Aiko gave him an eager nod. Dr. Arai, seemingly around Aiko's age, smiled and said, "See?" as if he were persuading a child. His tiny eyes narrowed into threads. Though he seemed a bit unctuous, he had a polite bearing and way of speaking.

"The procedure is called a facelift," said the director. "Simply put, it's a method of removing and tightening the skin."

Removing the skin. Aiko shuddered.

There was a knock on the door. A nurse wearing a pink uniform poked her head inside. "Excuse me, Doctor Arai. Mrs. Takeda's daughter is out of surgery. She'll be in the waiting area."

Minako was done already. Aiko reflexively checked her watch and confirmed that the surgery had indeed only taken 15 minutes. It was as simple that. And now Minako was in the waiting room, having altered the shape of her belly button.

"Your daughter will want to have a peek, but you'll have to remind her that she isn't to touch her navel for a week," said Dr. Arai to Aiko after the nurse left. "Now, about the facelift…"

In short, he would cut around the ear and alongthe hairline, remove the skin and muscle layers separately, and tighten the deeper muscle tissue underneath. The skin would be re-draped over the tightened muscle, so it would look even more natural with little strain on the skin. By tightening the entire face, the areas around the eyes, cheeks and mouth would become smoother. Because of Aiko's relative youth, she didn't have many wrinkles on her forehead. But if those lines became more prominent, the doctor would be able to tighten just that area using the same method.

"But keep in mind: you will look much younger for certain. In your case, I'd say about ten years younger. But this isn't some kind of magic. We can't stop time, so you'll need to continue caring for your skin, or you'll gradually go back to looking older again."

The doctor's explanation sounded very logical. In her mind, Aiko had already committed to having the surgery. However, there were a number of issues to consider. Aside from the cost, of course, how would she plead her case to her husband? Or would she be able to hide it from him altogether?

"How many days will I be in the hospital? Surely for such a major surgery—"

"Not necessary. It's different than navel surgery, so the procedure will take longer and you should expect some swelling afterwards, but that will subside in about three days. We'll remove the sutures and have you visit on an outpatient basis for a week to ten days to check up on your progress, just in case. You'll have to refrain from taking a bath or washing your hair for a while."

The assurance of check-ups gave Aiko a huge sense of relief. A facelift was certainly more serious than navel surgery. It would be unthinkable if the doctors told her to look after her own recovery. But since the director of the clinic was going to monitor her recovery himself, she was convinced she had nothing to worry about.

"Figuring in the cost of face treatments to prevent over-tightening and other such services, it will cost a little more."

"How much…?"

"Including consultations, tests and check-ups, anesthetics, medication, about 1,300,000 yen."

She had already dissolved one of her term deposit accounts in her mind. It was Aiko who held the family purse strings. But since their savings were naturally kept in the bank where her husband worked, he could always check on the family's finances online without her permission. Despite being trained to consult him about everything, and even though he'd said she was responsible for all household matters, Aiko hated the suffocating feeling of being kept on a tight leash. In fact, Aiko had secretly opened accounts in her own name at other banks and had been saving away money for years. She also had some money invested with a securities firm. Set aside for emergencies, these savings were products of her resourcefulness as a wife rather than a secret. Aiko had never bought anything that her husband didn't know about, and as long it was paid out of the established budget with his consent, he didn't have any reason to complain much about her purchases.

No, I can't!

It would set a bad example for the children. Aiko had raised her daughters to respect their father and to never keep secrets. If she were to violate those rules herself, she would lose their trust in a flash. Her older daughter, Chiharu, especially, might completely despise her.

Having heard so much about the procedure, however, Aiko was helpless against her own imagination, where she already saw herself rejuvenated. Although she never considered her family a waste of her time, she at least wanted to rid her face of any trace of the years she'd dedicated solely to their sake. She was still only forty-five, after all. Now that the children needed less attention, this might be Aiko's chance to start living her life as a woman again.

"Of course, we'll give you an anesthetic injection so you won't feel any pain. Why, we even have anesthetics for giving anesthetic injections for patients who don't cope well with pain. We'll also give you a hemostatic injection, so there's very little blood loss."

"But...I'll have to discuss it with my husband," said Aiko, belying her true feelings.

"Are you happily married?" Dr. Arai asked, his expression suddenly turning formal.

Aiko felt her face flush at such an abrupt question. "Well, he's very busy, you see—"

"You should make yourself attractive, Mrs. Takeda," said the doctor. "And then your husband will change, too." She had never considered such a scenario. Aiko smiled slightly and looked into the doctor's eyes, which again narrowed into threads. "Not just your husband. I'm certain other men will notice, too," he said, with a slightly lurid smile.

Aiko's heart pulsed a little faster. She recalled when she was younger, not yet sullied by the world. Would those days be brought back to her?

"What husband would be angry at his wife for making herself beautiful? When he compliments you on how beautiful you've become, then you can tell him about the surgery. He won't mind."

Yes, thought Aiko. She would be telling her husband *after* the fact, so she wouldn't necessarily be keeping secrets. But how would she explain the cost of the surgery?

"How about taking that next step? If you sit there worrying over it, you'll lose the courage you found thanks to your daughter. You'll be right back where you started." The director leaned back in his chair and smiled.

One million three hundred thousand yen. How was she going to explain where she had that kind of money? What if she told him that she'd been putting away what she could all these years for a facelift? But where? Under the mattress? No. She didn't want to risk the chance of her other accounts being discovered with a half-baked explanation.

"Well, Mrs. Takeda?" said the director, glancing up at the wall clock. The consultation fee was 5,000 yen per half hour. They'd already been talking for over 40 minutes. But what they were discussing was about a surgical procedure—cosmetic surgery, but surgery nevertheless. Was it wise to make such a decision so hastily?

Perhaps she'd better think through her options at home.

"Oh, and another thing—" said the director, shifting in his chair. "We've developed a cutting-edge technique called 'The Arai Method' that you won't see used anywhere else. Our motto here is: painless, speedy and beautiful. As I explained to you earlier, we begin by thoroughly eliminating our patients' fears and pain, such as by using anesthetics to dull the pain of anesthetic injections. Perhaps you'd like to visit some other clinics and see for yourself. It may be odd for me to say this, but I doubt you'll find the director of a clinic who is willing to counsel patients himself."

The director seemed to be misreading the reason for Aiko's indecision. Aiko nodded noncommittally.

"Furthermore, I believe 1,300,000 yen for everything is a reasonable price. I understand that some clinics are surprisingly cheap, sometimes charging as little as 500,000 yen. Such places can't be trusted."

"Oh...?"

"On the other hand, some clinics charge as much as 20,000,000. With the 'Arai Method,' we don't gouge our customers the way those other places do."

"I see."

"You happened to come here today because of your daughter. But let's say you go home and decide to do nothing. Years later, you may come to regret not having the surgery, but the opportunity will have passed. Our only wish is for women like yourself to go on living beautiful and vibrant lives."

Finally, Aiko consented. Though the doctor's persistence had certainly swayed her decision, in the end, she simply couldn't resist the temptation. She asked him to wait on scheduling the surgery until she could check her husband's schedule. The director countered that they should at least get the pre-surgery tests out of the way first.

"We do have our own schedule to consider," he said. "We take great time and care with these consultations, not to mention we're quite busy with surgical appointments."

He opened a thick appointment book and asked if Aiko was available on Wednesday. Having no set schedule to speak of, Aiko answered with a polite nod. She left the doctor's office, feeling a strange mix of hope and unease.

Aiko found her daughter sitting in the waiting room. "Well, how did it go?" Aiko asked.

Grinning, Minako answered that the surgery was over in no time and that she didn't feel a thing. After Aiko paid for Minako's procedure and her own consultation, the receptionist said, "See you next week," as they left the clinic. With the early summer sun beginning to set, the streets were flooded with people, with many young folks already walking around in midsummer fashions.

"That's what I'm going to be wearing soon," chirped Minako, glancing sideways at a girl in colorful pants and what looked like a bikini top or bra.

How obscene, thought Aiko, but said nothing, her head filled with thoughts of her own facelift.

"What about you, mom? What are you going to do?" Minako asked as they boarded the Inokashira Line train. Aiko vaguely tilted her head. "You're doing it, aren't you?" said Minako, after looking her mother dead in the eyes.

Aiko let out a deep sigh and answered, "Yeah, I guess I am."

"Whoa! Gutsy move, mom!"

"Really?"

"And dad can't find out about this, right?"

"Well, I doubt we can keep it from him. One look at me and he's bound to find out."

Gripping the straps overhead, mother and daughter stood side by side and continued their conversation in a whisper. Aiko explained how she planned to surprise her husband after she'd had the surgery, to which Minako grinned and said, "Uh-huh. I guess that's one way to do it."

Aiko felt cross with the conspiratorial way her daughter looked at her, but a bit ticklish and happy at the same time. *Soon I'll be rejuvenated. I'll have the kind of youthful skin that can't be had at a day spa.* The thought alone made her heart race. It was enough to make her giddy with joy.

4

Aiko's husband spent much of the year away on business. Several days after her consultation and before Aiko had much time to worry, he told her of a week-long trip to various regional branches starting next week.

"A week?"

"Maybe longer," he said. "I've been asked to play golf that Saturday and Sunday. I'll probably take the first flight back on Monday and go straight to the office from the airport."

"So you'll be back Monday the earliest."

"That's about right."

Offering her usual platitudes about how hard he worked, Aiko gazed at his back as he changed out of his clothes. *You're in for quite a surprise next week.* So absorbed was Aiko with imagining her rejuvenated self that she felt none of the guiltiness that she had initially anticipated. Minako's navel procedure was nothing compared to the surgery she was about to have. She felt a vague delight just thinking about it. Aiko had been squirreling away cash, even though she'd promised never to keep secrets. Regardless of the reason, there was no denying now that she was concealing something from her husband.

"This is a big step for you, mom," said Aiko's older daughter.

"Not you too, Chiharu," Aiko said.

"But it's true," said Chiharu with an amused look. "I didn't think you had it in you." Then she assured her mother that she knew how to keep her mouth shut, unlike *someone* she knew, and since she wouldn't be seeing her father much before the operation, there would be no chance of her ratting her out. And so, with the full-throated support of her daughters, Aiko made a surgical appointment on the same day that her husband would leave on his trip. She would be lying if she didn't admit feeling some anxiety, but Dr. Arai spoke to her very politely during the lab work and pre-surgical massage to try to smooth away her fears.

"You'll feel a prick for just a second. Good, now breathe out and relax."

Thus began Aiko's surgery on the very day she saw her husband off. The procedure was scheduled to take two and a half hours. Aiko lay on the operating table in the sterile OR, listening to the same ambient music that was playing in the waiting area, and imagined herself instantly younger upon sitting up.

"There, you see? No bleeding." Dr. Arai spoke to her occasionally, as the surgery went on. "Everything all right? We're nearly halfway through."

What must my face look like now? Aiko couldn't imagine what her face might look like with the skin peeled away. Thanks to the local anesthesia, she felt no pain yet remained lucid.

"What did I tell you, Mrs. Takeda? You're going to be beautiful." Dr. Arai began to talk in her ear just as she wondered if the worst of it was over. "If we could do something about your sagging eyelids, that would really take years off. More than ten years—a dozen or more years at least."

Eyelids? Come to think of it, I suppose you can't tighten the skin on the eyelids in the same way you can stretch the skin tighter across the face.

"If we also removed some of the fat under the chin, you'd be perfect. You were very beautiful from the start, Mrs. Takeda. It's a pleasure working on a face as beautiful as yours."

Listening as she did to Dr. Arai's flattery, Aiko emerged from the surgery ten minutes over schedule.

According to the director, the swelling would go down in three days. But five days had passed and the swelling on Aiko's face had still not subsided. Her entire face, marked by dark bruises, felt itchy and faintly feverish.

"Don't worry, these things vary with each patient." Dr. Arai made the same assurances every couple of days when she visited the clinic. "The incision lines look fantastic. Your recovery may take longer if you worry, so it's best you keep telling yourself that you'll be better and more beautiful soon."

But what if the pain and swelling doesn't go away? When she thought about her husband's imminent return, she could hardly relax. Nevertheless the discomfort gradually dissipated as if the layers of skin were being peeled away one by one.

On the day of her husband's return, the dressings and bandages came off and Aiko saw her face in the mirror for the first time.

"There, how lovely."

"They're gone." Aiko stared in the hand mirror and felt as if she were dreaming. The age lines along the sides of the mouth and carved around her eyes had disappeared. Her once-sagging cheeks were now firm. Letting out a deep sigh, she continued to gaze at her face. Dr. Arai asked how she liked it. Moved beyond words, Aiko could only nod.

Since she'd already made a deposit, she paid the remaining 1,000,000 yen and was done. Aiko bounded down the early-summer streets of Shibuya as if her whole body had been rejuvenated. Though the wind felt muggy and far from refreshing, even that made her irrepressibly happy. After all, dry air was the skin's worst enemy. This humid wind would only smooth her skin even more.

She found herself putting on an affected air, wondering whether someone might stop to take notice and recognize her youthful beauty. She wanted to go to a department store and buy a new outfit. She wanted to admire her younger self, alone in the fitting room. But her husband would return that day. She had neglected her household duties, having felt sluggish since the surgery. She would have to clean the house and prepare an elaborate dinner. And then she would witness her husband's shock. Desperately fighting back temptation, Aiko picked up only the necessary groceries and hurried home.

"Wow, mom, way to go!"

"Your skin looks so smooth!"

Minako and Chiharu came home from school and took turns peering into Aiko's face and exclaiming in surprise. Standing in the same old kitchen wearing her usual clothes, Aiko felt alive in a way she'd not felt since the girls were little.

"Let's not tell you father until he notices first."

"Of course he's going to notice."

"Yes, but still…" Aiko shot her daughters a mischievous look, as she hurriedly prepared dinner.

The girls nodded in an atypically obedient manner and smiled. "Dad's going to be blown away."

Just as the meal was prepared, the doorbell rang. Although Mr. Takeda was rarely home for dinner, it was his custom to return early enough for the evening meal the day he got back from his business trips. Minako went to greet him at the door. Aiko checked to see if anything was missing from the dinner table and casually fixed her hair.

She heard Minako greet her father at the door, followed by "Yay!" She smiled, figuring Minako had been handed a souvenir. Before long, the ever-tired figure of her husband stood in the dining room doorway. Seeing dinner already set out and Chiharu seated at the table, he grunted his surprise.

"Welcome home," said Aiko. "We've been waiting for you."

He gave a satisfied nod and went upstairs saying he wanted

to change out of his clothes. Aiko's heart sank a little. Maybe he'd been too far away to notice.

Mr. Takeda sat down at the table and opened the evening newspaper.

"Would you like some beer?"

He grunted his typical assent from the other side of the paper. Aiko hurriedly brought out a bottle and offered to pour the beer. He folded the newspaper, held out his glass, and looked up at Aiko for the first time.

"What's going on?" he asked.

In an instant, her heart began to pound. *Oh, I haven't felt this way in years! In decades!* "What do you mean?" she asked.

"You're being awfully attentive today."

Aiko smiled and slowly poured the beer. Her husband's eyes were unmistakably focused on her face. *Notice, please! Hurry! Tell me that I'm beautiful!* Setting the beer bottle on the table, she shifted her gaze to her husband, but he had already looked away. She glanced at her disappointed daughters, who'd been waiting expectantly to glimpse their father's reaction. Aiko sat back down timidly, not knowing where to bury her newly-revived excitement.

"Well, shall we eat?" Aiko fell silent, thinking the dinner rather pointless if her husband was not going to notice. Her daughters felt the same.

The dinner went on in an unusually awkward silence, until finally Minako blurted out, "dad."

"What?" he asked casually, looking at her.

"Don't you think there's something different about mom?"

He regarded Aiko's face as he chewed. Tilting his head to the side, he said, "Well…" Aiko's heart began to pound again. "Now that you mention it—"

Yes, don't I look younger? Like I did in the past?

"You look like you've gained weight."

Aiko was dumbfounded. Her daughters sat slack-jawed in disbelief.

"Over-snacking between meals, I bet. What happened to that dance school?"

"I stopped going," muttered Aiko. "Someone there isn't very nice."

"Again? You're a lion at home but a mouse outdoors," he sneered. "That's why you can never stick to any of your hobbies."

Suddenly, Aiko felt heartbroken. At the same time, she sensed anger beginning to boil in the pit of her stomach. There had to be something more he noticed. To begin with, she had quit dance lessons half a year ago. Why would he mention such a thing and not notice the transformation so plainly in front of him?

Mr. Takeda went about asking his daughters a few questions, to which the girls mumbled some listless answers so as not to provoke rebuke or get on his nerves. The dinner progressed in an unnatural quietness. After he slurped down his tea, Mr. Takeda announced that he was tired and left the table. All he would do now was take a bath and retire to the bedroom.

"I wonder why he didn't notice."

"Maybe dad's never really looked at her face before."

Aiko had no answers for her daughters. A bitter feeling of betrayal began to swell inside her.

5

A day passed. Then a week. Yet Aiko's husband had still not noted the change in her appearance. At first she was simply angry, but Aiko was soon confronted with a new worry: Perhaps she didn't look as young as she felt. If that were the case, she would have to attempt a more drastic change. Aiko promptly decided to fix her sagging eyelids. This particular surgery, unlike the first, would be faster and cost only 300,000 yen. She made an appointment on a day her husband would leave on business, as before, and returned to the clinic to have the excess folds on her eyelids removed and the skin tightened.

"Too much off the lower lids and they might turn outwards, but you'll see quite a difference with the upper lids alone. Now, if we sucked out the fat from under the chin, the double chin will be gone and you'll have a much prettier jawline," said Dr. Arai as he worked.

Several days later, Aiko's sleepy eyes were round and the lids creased just like when she was young.

"You're sure beginning to look like I remember you when you were young," her daughters took turns telling her, gazing at an old photo album. Yet her husband still failed to take notice. Except once, when he ask if she had changed her makeup. However, the remark that followed irritated Aiko very much:

"I guess, at this point, makeup wouldn't make a difference."

Just how ugly do you think I am? What husband could remain so oblivious to the changes in his wife of twenty years, the wife who'd borne him two children? Fine, then. I'll just have to get rid of the double chin. Aiko no longer wavered. In fact, by the end of the hot summer, she was practically defiant.

The standard method of liposuction was to break up the excess fat with ultrasound. On this visit to the clinic, Dr. Arai revealed that of all the procedures offered at the clinic, liposuction was his specialty. "We make an incision and suck out the broken up fat cells through a tiny tube. The incision is very small, about five millimeters."

The procedure would cost 350,000 yen. Aiko went straight to the bank and made a withdrawal from the nest egg that had taken years to save. Even though money could not really buy back her youth, it was money well spent if she could at least regain her youthful looks.

By the time the weather began to cool, Aiko had acquired a truly young face. Neighboring housewives and mothers of Minako's classmates began to take notice.

"I've seen you around town more often. You're looking young."

"Minako's mother looks so lovely!"

Every time Aiko heard such praises, she felt as if she were walking on air. One housewife even whispered in confidence, "You're not in love, are you?" Why was her husband the only one who hadn't recognized such obvious changes? She began to resent the man who noticed nothing and said nothing. *Jackass! Just how clueless and thickheaded can you be?* When she thought about how she'd looked after the household, having to ask his permission about the tiniest of matters, she wanted to scream.

Around the same time, Chiharu spoke up about wanting to alter her face. Aiko was more than a little surprised by this announcement.

"I'm in the most urgent situation of any of us. I have to a find job by this time next year, and the employment outlook for women is still dim."

With regard to Chiharu's employment, Aiko had asked her husband to put in a good word at the bank. However, Chiharu's first choice was something in the media. She insisted that even if she managed to land an employment exam through a personal connection, first impressions were crucial at the interview, which was why she wanted to fix the creaseless eyelids she inherited from her father and the flat button nose inherited from her mother. Aiko grimaced. What Chiharu was proposing wasn't like altering a concealed area like the navel or like defying age like Aiko. In fact, she was opting to change a feature that resembled her own. Aiko couldn't help feeling as if her own face were being criticized. Nevertheless, Chiharu had already made up her mind, and given that Aiko had been under the knife several times these past several months, it was difficult for her to say no to a daughter whose future was at stake.

"But even your father will notice those kinds of changes," said Aiko.

"Why don't we try it and find out?"

"But there's still some work I need done. Dr. Arai suggested that we remove the fat around my stomach, thighs, and arms."

"No fair! You're the only one getting prettier! Aren't you the least bit worried for you daughter's future?"

The truth was Aiko's nest egg was nearly zeroed out. The liposuction for the areas she was considering alone would cost two million yen, which was reason enough to have second thoughts. But she had to consider her daughter's future first. In addition, Chiharu promised that she would pay back the cost of her surgeries in installments after she found a job.

In the end, Chiharu won over her mother who accompanied her to Arai Clinic the following week. Conducting the consultation was a young doctor named Nakao, whom Aiko had not seen before.

"The eyes won't be too difficult, but the nose—might be best to bring in the nostrils and make the nose just a little bit higher so we retain the overall balance of your face," said Dr. Nakao, drawing a picture as he explained. To Aiko's surprise, Chiharu specified the desired size of her eyes, width of her creased eyelids as well as the height of her nose down to the millimeter. "It means that your daughter has a clear image of what she'd like, which is always preferable to the alternative," reassured the doctor. "It's the women that don't that are more troublesome."

Although the doctor didn't have an expressive face, he sounded sincere enough. It was decided Chiharu would have the surgery in three days. The cost for both procedures was 600,000 yen—a sum that would clean out Aiko's nest egg completely. But Aiko had already decided that if her savings were gone, she would simply dissolve another fixed-term deposit account. After all, who was going to notice? As much as her husband liked to say that he "trusted" her with all household matters, this was far from trust. It was neglect.

Three days later, against Chiharu's objections, Aiko accompanied her daughter back to the clinic. The surgery lasted roughly an hour. Afterwards, the eyelids were treated with ice for half an hour to reduce swelling, and then it was over.

"Don't you worry, it'll take a month to heal completely. Your mother knows the drill, so you're in good hands." The heavily made-up receptionist flashed her usual artificial smile. Aiko smiled back at the woman with whom she had become friendly over her many visits. The woman, whose features looked more European than Japanese, revealed that she had altered her eyes and nose, and shaved down her chin bone to make her face thinner. After Aiko paid for Chiharu's surgery, her nest egg was gone.

As a week passed into ten days, the swelling gradually receded from Chiharu's face. Once she had completely healed, the question became, when would her father notice? Even when he wasn't away on business trips, he'd been working late and had barely seen anyone in the family in weeks. Two weeks after Chiharu's surgery, however, he decided to forgo golf and spend a rare Saturday at home.

"Your father has the day off today. You girls hurry home tonight," Aiko told her daughters over breakfast before her husband had awakened.

"But I have plans tonight," said Minako, whose clothes had become more revealing since the navel surgery, probably thanks to a boost in self-esteem. The teen was getting calls at night and staying out late.

"Don't say that, please. And you too, Chiharu," Aiko said, turning to her older daughter, whose new face made her think she wasn't her own daughter at first. Now she had grown accustomed to it. "This is your chance to show him your new look. Just be back by dinner time."

"What if dad notices?" Even Chiharu couldn't hide her anxiety.

Aiko was rather amazed by how much more animated Chiharu's face seemed when she widened her eyes or looked down. Her higher, narrower nose also seemed to make her look more refined. "Well, of course he will. But the surgery was your decision, so you're going to have to talk to him yourself. I'll help you smooth things over with him, all right?"

Even if he did not notice Aiko's, he would have to notice Chiharu's transformation. How would he react when he does? Would he yell or be struck speechless?

Aiko spent a quiet Saturday with her husband, who spent the better of the day holed up in his study arranging books, at times going out in the yard to gaze idly at the garden. Although they shared a late breakfast, a light lunch and afternoon tea, her husband appeared not to notice any change in his wife. Aiko wanted to enjoy a proper conversation with her husband the way couples do. If he would notice, she might be able to do just that, maybe even tell him about Chiharu's surgery to soften the blow. But his gaze was always turned to the television, newspapers or the window. When he did speak up, what came out of his mouth were foreboding forecasts about the economy and how it was only going to get worse for the banks.

After they'd spent the entire day together, the man had failed to notice any change in his own wife. The more she thought about it, the more she was filled with disgust. It wasn't that he was busy, she finally realized. He simply didn't have any interest in her. *I always believed that he was the center of my life, the center of this family.* But their marriage was nothing more than a sham. Suddenly, Aiko recalled the very first consultation with Dr. Makabe. The young doctor had told her that the navel wasn't at all vital to the body—that despite being located in the middle of the abdomen, it was useless, nothing more than a scar.

As the day faded into evening, Aiko's husband came out of the study to read the mail and asked for a cup of tea. Aiko poured boiling water into the teapot and muttered, "You are the belly button of the family."

Saying nothing, he shot her a disapproving look for stating such an obvious truth. Aiko despised him for his ignorance of the true meaning of her words. She realized for the first time that she had married an idiot.

At dinner, Aiko's husband failed to notice the change in Chiharu.

"Anything new with you?" he asked his elder daughter.

Chiharu glanced at Aiko and answered that she was getting ready go on the job hunt.

"I see," he said and nodded, saying nothing more. Until a short while ago, such an attitude had been reassuring to Aiko. She had thought that the added girth that came with middle age even lent him an air of dignity. She was convinced now that it was all nothing more than a put-on.

If that was the case, what obligation did Aiko have to fret over a mere belly button? Aiko stared cooly at this loathsome man, as he yawned repeatedly as soon as he'd finished dinner and retreated to the bedroom for the night.

6

As the end of the year approached, Aiko's husband went on more business trips and grew even busier with the start of the new year. The lines carved between his brows growing deeper by the day, and he stopped talking not just to Aiko but to his daughters as well. It seemed he was facing difficulties at work. Given the financial turmoil in recent years, apparently the banks were bracing for another Big Bang. No matter what she said to him, such as, "Try not to work too hard," he only gave his usual empty response.

Aiko's husband habitually said that he would never bring his work home, so she needn't worry about anything else but to look after the house. Aiko chose not to be worried. If that was what her husband wanted, then Aiko was only too happy to oblige. Ultimately, this man lived in an entirely different space and time and had little interest in Aiko or his growing children.

"I'm going to see a play with a friend tomorrow," said Aiko. "Would you mind lending me one of your dresses?"

"Then can I borrow that suit you bought the other day?" asked Chiharu.

"For what?

"A date. With a businessman, so I want to look mature."

Spring gave way to the start of the rainy season. Since Minako wasn't yet home, Aiko and Chiharu ate dinner together as had become their custom and chatted about their plans. Suddenly, the sound of the rain hammering the roof of the house grew louder.

"It's really starting to come down," said Aiko, now looking

young enough to be mistaken for Chiharu's sister.

The doorbell rang. *That must be Minako. Did she beat the rain home?* Aiko went to the door. She was surprised to see her husband standing there.

"Oh... Welcome home."

It wasn't even nine yet. Aiko was flustered. She stared at her husband whose shoulders were dripping wet. His upper body swayed as he came through the door, reeking of alcohol. He staggered as he walked. He was never much of a drinker, so it was unusual for him to be so far gone.

"You're early." *How am I going to explain Minako not being home yet?* Aiko worried as she turned around.

Mr. Takeda sat down on the foyer step, slumped over with his elbows on his knees. She had never seen him like this. For a moment, Aiko didn't know what to do but stare down at him, until she heard a groan escape his down-turned face. "I'm done. I—I can't do it anymore..."

An inexplicable shiver ran down her spine. She was frozen, unable to even take a step towards him. *What did he say?* Never had Aiko heard such an admission of weakness from her husband. For a moment, she thought she might go crazy.

"Who is it? Dad?" said Chiharu in shock, peering out from the living room. The man was motionless. Aiko turned to her daughter and shrugged. They could hear the sound of rain pouring down outside the entryway.

"Is he sleeping? Is he okay?" Chiharu whispered.

"I think he's very drunk," Aiko whispered back.

Mr. Takeda remained slumped over, perfectly still. Aiko wondered how they were going to carry this large man upstairs, when the doorbell rang a second time. Quickly, she pushed open the unlocked door.

"It's really pouring out there!" Minako burst in giggling, her hair dripping wet. A humid wind blew in, dampening the floor.

Mr. Takeda groaned and raised his head. Letting out a heavy sigh, he slowly opened his eyes as if they were very heavy and tried to focus them. For several moments, there was a strange silence. His eyes wandered feebly until they found Aiko, Minako who had just entered, and Chiharu who stood peering at him over his shoulder. "Sorry, I didn't know we had guests," he said in surprise, his lips moving slowly. "Are you friends of Chiharu? Or Minako?"

Surrounded by his wife, so much younger and thinner that she was unrecognizable, his scantily-dressed younger daughter exposing as much of her limbs as she dared, and his sharply-featured older daughter, he repeated, "Excuse me... Sorry..." Then he slumped over again. "My wife, would you mind getting my wife?"

Chiharu was dumbstruck. Not knowing how to answer, Aiko could only stare.

"Please, I'm so tired. I can't seem to stand up."

Minutes later, he began to snore loudly. Surrounded by his family, he would never wake up again.

BLOOD

1

Fumiya was awakened by the sound of the *ping*. When he cast a bleary eye upward, the "fasten seatbelt" sign was turned on. A female voice announced the plane's gradual descent into Haneda Airport. He must have dozed off. After stretching a bit in the cramped seat, Fumiya pressed his forehead against the small, round airplane window. The world outside was shrouded in darkness. The blinking nightscape below grew denser by the minute, and soon, Tokyo's sea of lights would come into view like an overturned jewel box. Home at last. It had been a long day.

You understand, don't you? I need some more time.

Fumiya recalled the despair and irritation in Reiko's voice, as she sat there biting her lip, cradling Mitsuya in her arms.

"On an intellectual level, I understand. I do. But in here—" she muttered, pressing her right hand against her chest, sounding tormented. "In here, I just can't."

Staring at his only son sleeping in his wife's arms, it was all Fumiya could do to voice the question, "What about Mitsuya?"

"I don't know. It isn't like I want him to grow up fatherless." Reiko let out a sad sigh and cooed over the toddler, gently brushing his hair away from his tiny forehead. Her gaze fixed downward, she asked, "Was it my fault?"

Was it? Was I wrong?

Reiko's despondent voice lingered in his ear, even now, as Fumiya looked down at the city lights below. He was well aware of the words she so desperately wanted to hear. But when confronted with the question, he had a fleeting thought that maybe she *was* to blame.

"No. It was completely my doing, I know that," he answered nonetheless. "Look, I'm apologizing, aren't I? Would you please just come home?"

But Reiko just shook her head until the very end. "I don't want to be here that long, either. I haven't told my parents the truth, so they're getting all suspicious and keep badgering me to tell them what happened."

In the end, it was the same refrain: She wanted to wait until she was calmer to make a decision, she needed more time. There was little else Fumiya could say. At his wit's end, he stood up with his head hung low. His mother's face flashed across his mind, but Fumiya couldn't very well drag Reiko home kicking and screaming.

"Mom's worried about you, too," he said, in parting.

"Oh," muttered Reiko, shooting him an awkward look. "I feel horrible about putting your mother through this…"

"It's all right. I can handle her."

Reiko's parents had made arrangements for dinner, expecting Fumiya to spend the night. As he went to leave they rushed over to make him stay, but when Reiko said nothing to stop him from going, an uneasy look came over their faces. With his best effort at cordiality, Fumiya bowed to his in-laws for looking after Reiko and walked out with heavy steps, leaving his wife at her family home. At the time, it was still light outside. The days were longer this time of year, and the sun went down later in Fukuoka than in Tokyo.

The nightscape now spread beneath him like a shimmering ocean. Fumiya gazed idly and wondered about the lives represented by each and every one of those lights.

Could this possibly be the beginning of the end? Could a single misstep break off the life he had managed to forge? And if that should happen, it would just be Fumiya and his mother again, and then what?

As the nightscape grew larger outside the airplane window, Fumiya felt as if he were being swallowed whole by a sea of lights. Soon, a gentle bump signaled a safe landing at Haneda Airport, as scheduled. He resolved to leave the swirl of questions behind him in the sky and focus on present reality.

I'll need every ounce of energy to deal with mom.

Fumiya deplaned with the throng of passengers, rode the monorail, and then the train, feeling needlessly tense all the while—a feeling he could not suppress of late. He willed himself to stay focused, looking only straight ahead, and by the time he arrived at his destination, he was utterly spent with exhaustion.

When the light from his house came into view, it was already past nine. Fumiya closed the aged wooden gate behind him and slid shut the loose, badly rusty bar with a grating screech and the front door opened as if in response. Fumiya's mother poked her head out. "Are you alone?" she asked in a puzzled voice, craning her head to see if anyone was behind him.

"I'm hungry." Slipping past his mother at the door, Fumiya took off his shoes and went into the living room, while she trailed after him with an endless stream of questions. *What happened? Where is Reiko?* In reply, Fumiya held out the egg-noodle dessert he'd picked up at the airport. "Oh," she said and plucked the gift out of his hand, her eyebrows knit and her mouth in a frown.

In the time-worn living room lit by fluorescent lamps was a familiar scene from Fumiya's childhood: a sewing kit and board laid out on the year-round *kotatsu* heated table, along with some folded terrycloth stuck with pins in an orderly fashion, light blue chalk for marking patterns, and a thimble. A red felt pincushion, with half-used threads of all colors in a tangle threaded through countless shiny needles, resembled the back of a hedgehog.

"How rare."

"I'm making some dishcloths. I worry about the pins when Mitsuya is around, so I thought I'd make a bunch while he's gone," explained his mother. "Never mind that—why are you alone?"

"Why?" he muttered, picking up and examining the neatly folded towels with red and green stitching. "She wanted more time to think."

"Think about what? What is there to think about for two weeks?"

Fumiya's mother had no idea why Reiko went back to Fukuoka. Partly because Fumiya didn't want her of all people knowing and because Reiko had also demurred, "How am I supposed to face your mother and say that?" It was why his mother assumed Reiko had gone home out of selfishness. As badly as he felt for Reiko, he believed it was for the best.

"Now, how about something to eat?"

"Are you telling me they didn't feed you over there? What is going on?" The anger was palpable in her voice.

Without a word, Fumiya sat at his usual place at the table and stared at the tabletop. In a house without a separate dining and living area typical of modern homes, the *kotatsu* table, set in the living room that was contiguous with the narrow kitchen, had served as a communal area for just about every activity, starting with meals. It was only when his mother was sewing that Fumiya, as a youngster, was never to come near the table.

If you step on a needle, it enters your body and travels round and round, through the blood vessels until it sticks you in the eye or heart.

Fumiya had believed his mother's words for many years. Whenever his mother said that, he imagined the needle traveling inside his body. He could even feel a sharp pain move from one part of the body to the next, until finally, he imagined the needle shooting out of his eye and became totally terrified. Until he was around ten, he didn't dare go near the table until his mother had finished her sewing and took out a magnet from a sewing box to find any stray pins or needles on the floor. Upon closer look, the sewing board, still in use after all these years, was frayed around the corners, its surface paper worn with the inner cardboard exposed in places, seeming to reflect his mother's history inside this house.

Realizing that Fumiya would not offer an answer, she let out a heavy sigh and went to the kitchen. "There isn't much. I was expecting you to eat at their place—spend the night even," she said, returning with a dishcloth to wipe off the tabletop. As she began putting away the sewing tools, she sighed again. "Just what is making her so moody, anyway? If something is troubling her, she should come right out and say so. She's so stand-offish or something. She didn't let on a bit."

"Maybe it's baby fatigue," said Fumiya.

"But she gets plenty of help from me, and besides, I don't recall asking her to do anything so exhausting—Did Reiko say something to you?"

"She didn't say anything. She probably just wanted to relax at her parents' house for a change."

"Didn't she do enough of that when she went back to deliver the baby?"

"She just needed a break."

A look of hurt pride came over her face. "That makes it sound as if I'm overworking her or something," she said, furrowing her eyebrows even further. The truth was Fumiya's mother and Reiko had gotten along reasonably well until now; it was no wonder she was so cross. "Not even a phone call. What is she so unhappy about?"

Unlike Fumiya, his mother was outgoing and forthright, the type to open up to just about anyone. But when she got bent out of shape, it usually took some time to recover her good mood.

Fumiya was well aware that when she knit her brows this way, he was in trouble. He had promised Reiko to smooth things over with his mother, but it was difficult to think that her mother could be persuaded of anything when she believed the daughter-in-law she'd come to care for had betrayed her.

"You know, she seemed worried. She said she felt horrible about putting you through this and that she was sorry for acting selfishly."

"Then why doesn't she tell me herself? Is there anything more unnatural?" she said angrily from the kitchen. "She suddenly ups and leaves, and then nothing for two weeks... It's just not right."

Fumiya ate the boiled vegetables, salt-cured salmon and pickles set before in him in silence. His disgruntled mother sat down across from him and prepared tea with her still-thimbled hands.

After a while, she asked, "How is Mitsuya?"

Fumiya recalled his son in Reiko's arms and replied that he was the same as always. There was nothing more he could say.

"Oh..." His mother nodded, dissatisfied. "I understand why she'd want to take Mitsuya, so her parents can spend time with their darling grandson, but it's been so lonely without him."

She stared wistfully at the newly-sewn dishcloths. Fumiya's mother, who for years had worked as a seamstress to support the family, believed that dishcloths had to be sewn by hand because they felt instantly familiar and comfortable. She had sewn countless terrycloth toys and stuffed animals for Mitsuya with her own hands, pointing out that it was an entirely different feeling compared to when she had been working against a deadline, sewing garments for people she didn't know.

"So? When will they be back?"

"Soon" was the only answer Fumiya could give.

"Fumiya," she said, pressing a new dishcloth against her cheek. "You two aren't thinking about...separating?"

"Of course not," Fumiya muttered, dropping his eyes on the teacup she slid in front of him. At least, *he* wasn't thinking about it. "You're worrying over nothing, mom."

No doubt, Reiko was trying to sort through her feelings to avoid a divorce.

"Then why doesn't she just come back?"

As his mother continued to mutter her displeasure, Fumiya wolfed down a late dinner he could hardly savor.

2

Two weeks ago on his way to work, Fumiya was stopped by the police. He had gotten off the train at the usual stop and started walking when someone grabbed his shoulder from behind.

"What were you doing just now?"

Fumiya turned around to find a small man with penetrating eyes. As he started to speak, Fumiya tried shaking him off, but the man grabbed his arm this time and said, "I'm with the police," in a low voice.

In that instant, Fumiya's mind went blank. Ears ringing, he felt his heart shrivel coldly in his chest. "I didn't do anything," he said in a voice that sounded strangely distant, but the patrolman only stared, stone-faced.

"I was there right beside you. I saw everything."

"Saw what?"

"What you did, of course. Now, why don't you come with me."

Fumiya recalled arguing back and forth for a while, until the patrolman's partner had come along and said, "The victim says you're the one that did it."

Fumiya felt his entire body freeze and that he might pass out. After an hour at the on-site railroad police station that he never knew existed, Fumiya had been coerced into declaring loudly, "I did it."

"Tell me what you did."

"I touched a woman."

"You didn't just touch her, now did you?"

"I touched her buttocks," said Fumiya, his body shaking with humiliation.

The interrogating officer sneered victoriously, patting Fumiya on the back. "You should've just said so. Just obediently admit what you did from the beginning."

"I'm sorry."

"Plus, you didn't just touch her, did you? You pressed up and rubbed your privates against her, didn't you?

"I'm sorry," said Fumiya, nearly in tears from shame. *No one should be humiliated in this way,* he thought.

The office spat out, "Pathetic," and told Fumiya that he was being arrested.

Fumiya's rapidly freezing heart began to beat furiously, sending the blood rushing to his head. "I'm being arrested?"

"Well yeah, you've committed a helluva crime. Isn't that right?"

"I—I won't do it again. So please, just let me—"

"Well, I would hope you wouldn't! But this is out of my hands. You aren't some kid, you understand. If people got off by saying they're sorry, then everyone would want to try something just once. And by the looks of you, this wasn't your first offense."

"Please—"

"You can't expect to keep up such bad behavior. You have a wife and kid, don't you? You know better than to pull such pathetic crap."

There was no use protesting. He was being arrested, but if there was a guarantor, he would be allowed to go home. Though he hated the idea of anyone seeing him in such a state, anything was better than being detained at the station. Fumiya reluctantly gave his wife's name and home phone number. The only thought racing through his head was how his mother could not know and how he didn't want to strike a blow to the image she had of him, even if he had to lie about his mother's health. "Talk to my wife, please," he pleaded. "My mother has high blood pressure and a bad heart, so she can't find out about this. Say that you're a friend or something, I'm begging you."

Perhaps the seemingly heartless, merciless detective was moved by Fumiya's desperation. A couple of hours passed, and his wife came running.

"What's going on?" Reiko muttered, staring straight ahead.

Reiko had left Mitsuya with Fumiya's mother and lied about a sick friend and left home. She didn't say a word until they boarded the train back. It was only when the familiar landscape passed outside the window and the train noise drowned out the people around them that she finally spoke. Her profile was pale and impenetrable like a Noh mask. "How could you, of all people... A groper..."

The word pierced Fumiya's brain like a knife. The sway of the train usually felt comfortable, and the post-rush hour train had a relaxed atmosphere. The word "Groper" sounded like it belonged to someone else entirely.

Groper. Groper.

Fumiya felt on the verge of crying out, *No! I didn't do anything so lewd, so vile!* Mindful of the people around him and Reiko staring out the window with her jaw clenched, however, Fumiya could say nothing. Given how suspicious it would look for the couple to return home together, Fumiya got off at the station near home, called the office to apologize for being late, and boarded an in-bound train.

That night after Fumiya had barely managed to keep up appearances at work and after his mother had gone to bed, Reiko confronted him in tears. "Why do you have to touch other women? Are you that sexually frustrated?" Her eyes were filled with obvious disgust as well as a certain kind of fear.

"No," Fumiya groaned, as if the word had to be wrung out of

his throat. "That's not it."

He explained in desperation that train was been crowded and that his body just happened to be pressed against the back of the woman standing in front of him. However, this explanation did nothing to change Reiko's expression. Eyeing him as if he was something dirty, she reasoned that his hand couldn't have found its way into the woman's skirt no matter how crowded the train might have been. He was shocked to discover that the police had told her everything.

"And do you know what else they said? That you were targeting a particular type of woman before you boarded the train. And that you wandered the platform for almost twenty minutes and deliberately got on a crowded train. How is that just an accident?"

Fumiya nervously dropped his shoulders. So he'd been spotted even before he boarded the train. "This is all a misunderstanding," he said, his voice fading feebly. He felt his stomach tighten with shame far worse than what he'd felt at the police station.

"I don't believe it," sniffled Reiko, tears continually streaming down her cheeks. "I'd understand if I'd been called to the station because you'd been in a fight. But why this? Why groping, of all things?"

It was true she'd been more tired since Mitsuya was born, so she might have neglected Fumiya from time to time, Reiko admitted. Even so, she asked, why did he have to relieve his sexual frustration in this way?

The following day, Reiko went home to Fukuoka with Mitsuya in her arms while Fumiya was at work. Every day for two weeks, Fumiya called her from the office. However, Reiko's voice was always despondent and her responses blunt regardless of what he said.

Perhaps it *was* groping. But in Fumiya's mind, what he'd intended was the world's shortest romance—one which achieved full bloom in an instant. A bittersweet romance that was heart-breaking and pure, and could never be realized. As inarticulate and inconspicuous as Fumiya was, it was also a rare moment to connect with his own primal nature, to remember his manliness.

What Fumiya loved were women's knees. When or how he'd become so infatuated with them he did not know. But before he knew it, every time he spotted a woman walking with her knees exposed, his heart raced and he was seized with the impulse to grab hold of them.

Every time he laid eyes on a pair of round knees with a little fat on them—unlike the bony, protruding kneecaps of a man—Fumiya felt an unadulterated happiness and sadness at the same time. There was no part of the body more captivating or precious as the backside of a woman's knees. For Fumiya, those dimpled knees, from the crease running across their back to the fat around the inside, were the object of his eternal longing.

The first time he gave in to his impulses was long before he ended up with Reiko. He happened upon a pair of supple-looking knees in the crowd waiting in line for the train. *What beautiful, lovely knees,* he'd thought. And before he knew it, he had boarded the train from the same door in pursuit of them.

When he came into contact with another man's knees on a crowded train, they only felt hard and knobby, even through pants. Their rough, unyielding stubbornness offended him. But a woman's knees had felt entirely different. Fumiya, who was taller than the average woman, had stood near his female target and casually bent his knees ever so slightly to brush against hers. He could not forget the ecstasy, the pure exhilaration he'd felt, even now.

Since then, every time he saw a woman walking on the train platform with her knees exposed, he made a point of touching them on the train. As he brought his knees closer to hers in time with the sway of the train, he imagined himself falling on top of the anonymous woman. So intoxicating was the fantasy of resting his head on those round, smooth knees, drawing them near and kissing their backs that Fumiya could feel the blood rushing through his body.

In repeating this exercise several times, Fumiya made one discovery: Women didn't think it particularly strange when their knees were touched. They were all, in fact, tolerant of Fumiya's actions, which perplexed him and made him even bolder. Over time, he came to believe that, despite how demurely they acted, women were in search of pleasure, too—that they dreamt of losing themselves in an intoxicating liaison with a random passerby, in the same way he imagined peeling off their clothes and caressing their knees to his heart's content. The very thought excited Fumiya even more, and soon his transgressions escalated.

When Fumiya bent his leg to touch the knees of a woman, his hips dipped lower, at times nestling against her buttocks, depending on how crowded the train was. Even if what he wanted to touch were her knees, if he moved his knees up and down, his hips naturally followed. As he repeated this undulating motion several times, the fantasy inside his head swelled into the delusion that he might have all of her.

Later, Fumiya met Reiko at a friend's wedding. She was tall, slender, fragile-looking, and at 27, eight years younger than Fumiya. She was an uncommonly modest and tolerant woman with a sensible head for her age, the kind of woman that was perfectly suited to live with his mother after they were married. And since his mother seemed to take an instant liking to her, Fumiya, already 35 at the time, decided quickly to marry her. Unlike his younger brother who had married young and already left home, Fumiya had always been shy and a cause for worry, so his mother rejoiced over the decision.

"I'm so relieved to have such a wonderful girl become a member of the family. I guess good things do come to those who wait."

Fumiya had resolved to cherish the woman whom his mother adored. But her slender body did not feel soft in his arms. Her knees were not the round, plump ones he yearned for.

It is what it is.

It wasn't like he was marrying Reiko's knees after all, and an attractive pair of knees certainly didn't promise a life of happily ever after. Thus Fumiya learned to separate his peaceful family life from his secret pleasure.

3

The week after Fumiya's failed trip to Fukuoka, Reiko returned home with a slightly unpleasant look on her face. "Mitsuya! Mitsuya!" Fumiya's mother lifted the boy ecstatically into her arms, but her attitude toward Reiko had completely changed.

"I'm not about to say you can't go visit your parents. But what were you thinking by leaving for three weeks without so much as a word?" Fumiya's mother held Mitsuya on her lap and shot Reiko a frigid look. It was the first time in three weeks that the family was sitting around the *kotatsu* table again. "Maybe you're a little full of yourself because Fumiya is always so quiet."

"Mom, let it go," said Fumiya in an attempt to intervene, which only succeeded in irritating his mother.

"This is why she takes you for granted," his mother declared.

For the first time since she had married into the family, a defiant look came into Reiko's eyes.

Damn it, I can't risk angering Reiko here. If she says, "Your son isn't all gentleness and kindness, mom. He was arrested for touching another woman's ass on the train," I'll lose everything. Sandwiched between the two women, Fumiya could only listen nervously to the exchange.

"Talk to me, Reiko, please," said his mother. "It doesn't feel right keeping secrets from each other living under the same roof. Why did you—"

"I'm sorry," said Reiko flatly.

"Well, you don't have to apologize. That's not why we're having this discussion. You didn't do anything you have to apologize for, did you? I'd just like a reason, is all."

"My father—hasn't been feeling well lately. I was worried, so…"

"Oh, for heaven's sake. Your father is ill? Why would you keep something so important from me? Think of how uncaring we must look to your parents that we haven't sent condolences!"

"Oh, no, it isn't that serious."

"If it isn't serious, then why have you been away for three weeks? Don't lie to me, Reiko."

"Knock it off!" Fumiya shouted. Startled by his own voice, he glanced back and forth at the two women for a moment before hastily looking down. His face turned crimson red. "She just went home to let her hair down for a bit. What's wrong with that?"

"And you're all right with that?" said his mother. "She's a member of *this* family now. And you allow such selfish behavior—"

"Will you shut up? Stop going on and on with your outdated ideas!"

This time, an unmistakable look of shock came over his mother's face, followed by heart-breaking despair. Fumiya couldn't help but look away.

His mother's life could hardly be called blessed. Fumiya's father had a violent streak when he drank and made his mother cry all too often. On top of which, she'd told Fumiya countless times that she was always apologizing to someone over the trouble her husband had caused, usually having to do with women and money. He died, eventually done in by drinking, when Fumiya was in third grade. Since then, Fumiya had never once raised his voice to the woman who had single-handedly raised him and his younger-by-four-years brother. They fought occasionally, of course, but compared to his brother Kazuya, who acted and said as he pleased, Fumiya was always the peacemaker, the pacifier. Silently, he had pledged that he would never be the one to hurt this woman who worked part-time at a neighborhood store during the day and sewed dresses at night to provide for the family.

"*Outdated*? Are you saying my opinions are just annoying?" She stared at him in disbelief, then shot a vicious look at Reiko. "You hear it all the time, you just never think that it would happen to you. You struggle and toil to raise a son, but once he's married, he's completely henpecked. I didn't imagine you'd be the same way."

"That's not how it is—"

"No, no, I don't mind. She's your wife. If you say it's all right, it's not my place to complain, outdated as I am."

Fumiya held his tongue, as a painful thought spread through him. Just when he thought the family was together again, that happier, more peaceful days would return with Mitsuya around, both his mother and Reiko fixed hard gazes at the floor, making it abundantly clear that there would be no going back.

That night when they were alone, Reiko confronted Fumiya in a way she never had before. "You're not doing it anymore, are you?"

"Of course not."

"You sure?"

"I'm sure. The devil made me do it just that once, that's all."

The truth was Fumiya hadn't touched another woman since he was arrested. Whenever he spotted a girl in a miniskirt, he deliberately averted his eyes, passing much of the time staring up at the sky, unnaturally tense. But Reiko, seemingly not totally convinced, let slip a small sigh.

"I'll let it go this time—but just this once," said Reiko. Her voice was resolute and unwavering as if to say that she would not hide it from his mother and end the marriage if he slipped again.

"I'm sorry." Fumiya bowed his head, choking back his humiliation.

"I don't care whether your mother knows or not. I don't know what I'll say if she ever talks to me like that again."

"Look, she spoke that way because she was worried about you."

"I thought you were going to smooth things over with her." Was Reiko always so cold, this harsh with her words? Fumiya doubted his own ears. He cast a wary glance at his wife, whose cheeks looked more sunken than before. She instantly knotted her brows in irritation. "If you don't pull yourself together, this really could be the end for us."

"I understand."

"What you did was the greatest humiliation not only to me but to all women. I haven't completely forgiven you yet."

Reiko went on to declare that she would rather have a cheater for a husband than a pervert. Fumiya could barely believe it. It wasn't like he had slept with any particular woman. He merely wanted to feel the pulse of life in his veins through a fleeting make-believe romance. Could she not allow him even that tiny pleasure?

"Tell me the truth," she continued. "Am I really that unattractive?"

"What?"

"You haven't touched me since Mitsuya was born. I thought it was for my sake because I've been so tired, but was I wrong? What sort of woman was she that made you want to…touch her?"

He couldn't answer it was a girl with round, soft kneecaps. He couldn't possibly tell this woman that that was the sort of girl who might nestle against him the moment he drew near.

"Fine. Then tell me this. Where's the turn-on in doing something like that?

"There's no turn-on. Like I said, it was just a momentary lapse."

There was no way Reiko would understand. The pleasure, in that instant, of feeling the blood rushing through his body, and that the world was filled with bare-kneed women that could make him feel this way.

Reiko's bony knees were thrust out in front of him. Even through the flower-patterned dress draped over her legs, Fumiya could make out their shape as well as her thin, fleshless thighs. Why couldn't they be rounder, more supple? Then Fumiya would caress those knees for the rest of his days. Yes, he would love them more than anything in this world.

"Anyway, I'm glad you're home." He extended a cautious hand for want of even the slightest thrill, only to have Reiko's sinewy hand brush it aside. A chill spread from his temples to the base of his neck.

"No," she said hoarsely, sitting up straight. "I told you. Intellectually, I understand. But I can't…"

"It's okay," said Fumiya, balling his spurned hand into a fist against his thigh. What else could he say? He had brought this upon himself. He had been the one to hurt Reiko.

On the surface, life went back to the way it was. The familiar sound of Mitsuya crying and laughing filled the run-down house Fumiya's father had left behind, while Fumiya's mother and Reiko fussed over him, cooing, "now, now" and "there, there." Fumiya went to work toward the goal of remodeling the house into a duplex by the time Mitsuya started kindergarten.

"What time will you be home tonight?"

"The usual time."

"Have a good day."

So was the extent of the morning conversation. Even after rejecting Fumiya's advances, Reiko saw him off every morning with Mitsuya in her arms. Fumiya made a point of waving before turning the corner and heading for the train station. Occasionally, he felt her gaze on his back; a dripping gaze that menaced, *Don't do anything stupid. Don't you dare grope anyone again.* It hung over him, and Fumiya spent the day carrying the weight of Reiko's scorn on his shoulders.

Will I ever feel that surge of blood in my body again?

He was gutless—Fumiya knew that about himself. After getting arrested and enduring such huge humiliation during the questioning, he hardly had the courage to touch another woman, even without Reiko's warning.

At night, there was scarcely anything resembling a conversation. Fumiya was an accountant at an office that rarely required overtime until the end of the fiscal term. With colleagues either saddled with growing kids and home loans or having to commute long distance, Fumiya only went out to drink once a week at most. Otherwise, he went home in time for dinner and watched TV or read the paper in timid silence, practically willing himself to shrink in size, before turning in for bed.

The truth of the matter was the mood inside the house had deteriorated dramatically since his wife returned. Though he had no idea what Reiko and his mother talked about while he was away at work, one step inside the house, he could sense whether they had merely bickered or fought viciously that day. Yet neither said anything about the other to Fumiya. In fact, they ignored Fumiya entirely, vying instead for Mitsuya's affection, the poor boy caught between them, as they exchanged mock pleasantries.

Maybe my blood will eventually run dry, Fumiya thought, passing each insipid day after the next, sitting at the same *kotatsu* table, going to work, only to go home to take a bath before retiring for the night. As long as the goal of remodeling the house hung over him and his mother held the purse strings, even after his father passed away, Fumiya couldn't indulge in any hobbies. Not yet 40, he began to feel as if all pleasure was already behind him.

BLOOD

No diversion was as instantly gratifying or as easy on the pockets as fleetingly touching a woman on the train, and the end to that dream left him deflated. Six months became a year, and Fumi-ya had given up on everything. Such was life. Was there ever any need to feel such primal urges or his blood flowing? He came to believe that everything was fine as long as the days passed without incident.

4

"Ouch!"

It was a muggy day toward the end of rainy season. With Fumiya's mother on a rare trip away with a friend for the weekend, Reiko strutted around the house as she pleased. Fumiya sat gazing at the yard, while he played with Mitsuya, who'd grown mischievous of late.

Suddenly Reiko had cried out behind him. Fumiya turned around to find her doubled over on her knees next to the *kotatsu* table. "I think I stepped on something," she whimpered. She squinted at the back of her foot and gasped. She held one hand up in front of her eyes. Something thin and sharp glinted between her fingers.

"What is it? Are you all right?" Fumiya went to her on all fours, like an infant. There was a silver sewing needle pinched between her fingers. "Did you step on it?" he asked, looking up to see her frowning and glowering at the needle.

"Damn it!" she cursed, thoroughly pissed off. "It's your mother. Why can't she be more careful with Mitsuya around?" Fumiya peered down in shock to the underside of her foot which she was gripping with one hand. She was not wearing socks as she had since early spring, probably wanting to spend the warmer months barefoot. On the bottom of her slightly dirty foot at the base of one big toe was a ruby-colored bead. The drop of red blood made Fumiya's heart jump the moment he saw it. How beautiful and sensual the color!

"She makes a big display of her sewing because I don't know

how to sew. What if Mitsuya had stepped on this needle or, God forbid, put it in his mouth?" After nearly a year of silence, the accusations against his mother poured out of her mouth as if a dam had broken, but Fumiya barely heard her. *So very red…* Sliding his body closer to hers, he leaned his face closer to her leg.

"She's the one always saying how dangerous needles are, and this is what happens! Fumiya—!"

Fumiya, his mind going blank, licked the blood drop from her foot with the tip of his tongue. The faint whiff of rust titillated his nasal cavity, sending his heart into palpitations. It was as if a drop of fresh energy had been absorbed into his body. When he pulled away, a slightly deformed drop was already beginning to form on the back of Reiko's spit-dampened foot. Fumiya leaned in again.

"Don't," said Reiko, sounding shocked, embarrassed and strangely sensual at the same time. "It's dirty." Fumiya looked up into her face. "What do you think you're doing?" she asked, leaning back. Despite her words, she looked enraptured.

In a flash, Fumiya pushed her down onto the tatami floor. A fierce exhilaration coursed through his body for the first time in a long while, as his tongue still tingled from the softness of her skin, the skin of a woman he'd thought was all skin and bones with no soft plumpness at all.

"Wait, wait," she gasped, as she lay pinned down. "Not here."

"It's all right," he answered, overcome with the same excitement he'd experienced on the crowded train. With his mother gone and Mitsuya playing in the hall, they were free to do as they pleased. Outside the window it was raining heavily, and he caught a glimpse of the adjacent house past the small yard and poorly groomed trees. "Careful, someone might see us," Fumiya whispered in her ear cruelly. Reiko's body twitched and tensed in his arms.

"No… Stop it, please…"

"You really want me to stop? Do you? Just how long do you think you've neglected me? I can't be held responsible if you ignore me for too much longer." Pressing his lips against the slightly damp nape of her neck, he continued to whisper, sliding one hand lower. Reiko swung her head from side to side, until soon, her body began to respond.

The blood flowing through my veins! Racing through my body at this very moment. Never had he wanted to make love to her as much as he did now—and he knew it was all instigated by a single drop of blood.

"You're not doing it anymore? You've stopped, haven't you?" Reiko asked, breathless. "Tell me that I'm the only one."

Fumiya's heart went cold in an instant. Reiko looked up at him with liquid eyes with her arms clasped firmly around his back. After staring into her face for a moment, he pulled away and sat cross-legged beside her.

"You don't trust me," he groaned. Reiko sat up, stunned, and with the front of her dress undone and hiked up to her waist, shot him a needy look. "You still don't trust me, is that it?" Fumiya said again.

"But you said—"

"You don't trust me, just say it!" he cried. In truth, he wasn't all that angry, but he needed some way to cover up the fact that he'd gone limp.

"I'm sorry, I'm sorry..." Reiko said, pressing her flushed face against him. "It's been hard for me, too. Ever since last year. I've missed you..." Fumiya mechanically put his arms around her and stroked her hair, staring at the raining pouring down. Was that all the energy that a single drop of blood could muster? "It's true," she continued. "The thought of you touching another woman, much less on a train, makes me crazy."

"All right. Let's not keep bringing up the past."

The bead of blood had been exquisite, like a jewel. And tasted of rust. Fumiya tried to revive that flavor in his mind, wanted to savor that faintly raw smell lingering inside his nose.

At that moment he finally realized: Fumiya was attracted to women's knees even now. How he yearned to lose himself in the recesses of a woman's soft flesh. But the truth was he didn't find much pleasure in thrusting himself into any sort of interlude only to have it conclude. This was why brushing up against a stranger on the train was easier and so much more comfortable and satisfying than making love to his wife. It was because the pursuit had no end that he did not tire of it.

What Fumiya desired was an invigorating encounter that would get his blood coursing through his body. He wanted to feel alive, awaken the primal instincts hidden away in the deepest part of him. If he couldn't, Fumiya could only think of himself as a scarecrow made of straw or mechanical doll—like how he'd felt this past year, a robot programmed to work tirelessly and want nothing else but his mother's happiness, a stable home, Mitsuya's growing older, and his wife's smile.

"Mitsuya, no!" Reiko let out. There was a noise from the hall, prompting her, nestled next to him like a puppy, to get up.

"You should disinfect that," he said, looking at his wife as she walked away, fixing the hem of her dress and buttoning up her blouse.

"I will," said Reiko over her shoulder, smiling bashfully. She tamed her tousled hair and trotted away.

After the weekend passed, the daily grind of work resumed.

"Have a good day."

After Fumiya had spent the weekend making love to her enough times to make up for a year, Reiko saw him off with a coy smile reminiscent of when they had first been married. Fumiya returned a cheerful smile. No doubt she had interpreted Fumiya's transformation as a complete change of heart, believing that the house would go back to being peaceful and happy like it used to be. And as her mood improved, so too did his mother's.

Nothing beats a happy home.

Now he could finally be alone. Just thinking about getting lost in his own world made his steps lighter. Fumiya tried to control himself as he headed for the train station with long, purposeful strides. Hidden inside his jacket pocket was a sewing needle he had taken from his mother's sewing box. Over the weekend, in private, he had fooled around pricking his own fingers and had arrived at one conclusion. In order not to be mistaken for a groper and still be able to enjoy some modicum of pleasure, he would have this needle nestle against a woman's body in his place.

5

Nearly a month passed before the news reported a rash of young women being pricked through their clothes by needles during the morning and evening commute. After an unusually long rainy season had finally ended, the Kanto region was suffering daily from sweltering heat.

"...six incidents reported since the middle of last month on the JR Yamanote line, Keihin Tohoku line, and the Marunouchi subway line. Sewing needles have been used in each of these incidents and stuck into the blouses or skirts of several female passengers. Because these needles can cause injury to the women as they move as well as passengers nearby, police are regarding these incidents as malicious pranks and are warning the public to beware..."

It was surreal. Incidents with which Fumiya was intimately familiar were being reported over the airwaves. There was no way Fumiya himself could see where the needles had ended up or witness the red bead of blood form on their skin. Other than relish the act of sticking the needle in, all he could do was imagine the rest. Never in his wildest dreams did he image that he'd be able to hear the subsequent details in such a titillating way.

"The heat certainly does bring out the weirdos," muttered his mother, staring fixedly at the television.

"Right," Reiko chimed in. Just as Fumiya had predicted, peace was restored to the household. Ever since that weekend, Reiko's irritation gave way to confidence, and she regained her usual calm and tenderness toward his mother. As Reiko's attitude changed, his mother naturally softened as well. In fact, his mother had always approved of Reiko as his wife more than he did.

"I wonder what fun there is in doing such a thing," Reiko asked.

"You never know what people are thinking nowadays," answered his mother. "And you know what? He probably looks as normal as you or me."

Sipping the one beer he allowed himself a day, Fumiya regarded Mitsuya playing with his food, then Reiko and his mother, and let out a chuckle. Reiko smiled back at him.

Who knew that a tiny needle could bring this about! Fumiya was satisfied. Every time he struck, he always blended into a crowded train and exercised the utmost caution so as not draw anyone's eye. The immediate excitement he felt upon plunging that silver needle into the woman's clothing without touching her and going wholly undetected was far greater than when he'd been targeting knees.

"Oh, maybe that's what I saw the other day," he said casually, holding his beer glass in one hand. When Reiko and his mother shot him a surprised look, he proceeded to fabricate a story about how he'd heard a woman scream in pain one morning on the train.

"That must've been it. You were there? Well, how about that." Though his mother seemed impressed at first, her lips quickly curled into a frown. "Now, I know you're thinking you don't need to worry since only young women are being targeted, but Fumiya, you need to be careful. You never know where trouble is lurking."

"Yes, but you can't guard against everything—random slashers, for instance."

"Be careful just the same. Mitsuya has his whole life ahead of him, and this family's future is all on your shoulders."

"That's right, papa," Reiko said, looking at him very seriously.

"Please be careful."

"Pa-pa," said little Mitsuya, mimicking Reiko.

Reiko had gotten into the habit recently of calling him "papa." Apparently his mother had advised her that by calling him such Fumiya would come to think of himself more as a father.

"Mother thinks you might be feeling a bit in the dark with regards to Mitsuya because you didn't have much of a relationship with your father... Because you probably don't have many memories of being loved," Reiko explained later that night in their bedroom.

Certainly, Fumiya had scarcely any memory of his father showing affection toward him. But he'd never felt deprived of anything. His mother had always protected and loved him, and that was enough. "I know how she's a worrywort."

"Only where you and Mitsuya are concerned." Lying next to Fumiya with a summer blanket over her stomach, Reiko flashed a mischievous look and added, "Right, *papa*?" Fumiya felt discomfited. Reiko seemed to say too much of late.

The household harmony had indeed been restored, perhaps even improved, as Fumiya no longer felt the need to gauge the temperature of the house every time he returned from work. At the same time, Reiko appeared to be undergoing some changes herself, becoming more assertive, pushy even, about trying to change the mood of the house to her taste. Fumiya bristled at the thought of her changing the house he and his mother had protected and grown accustomed to for so long.

"Better not say anything to worry your mother, right?" With this, Fumiya shot her a sidelong glance and turned over on his side. She asked innocently from behind, "You're not mad, are you?" but he didn't feel like answering.

Maybe tomorrow at this rate. Fumiya had made a point of giving himself the "green light" when something at home or at the office soured his mood, even if he was simply drained from sighing all day and not particularly pissed off. Without these self-imposed limitations, he was afraid he'd end up carrying a needle every day. Plus, it would keep him within bounds and help him avoid getting arrested again.

"Hey."

"Yeah."

"Do you love me?"

"Yeah."

"You know what?"

"Hmm?"

"Mother was asking if we planned to keep Mitsuya an only child."

"…"

"And that we need to make sure our kids graduate college before you retire."

"…"

"I have to agree with her. You got married late. It's something you should give some serious thought to."

"Yeah." He wasn't opposed to giving her another grandchild or two if that was what his mother wanted. But what he couldn't tolerate was that Reiko was trying to seduce him in this way. She seemed to him shameless, lustful, even lewd.

"So why don't we—"

"I'm going to sleep." Turning his back to Reiko, folded his arms and shut his eyes. He heard her mutter, "Okay…" before turning off the small orange nightlight. Reiko let out a heavy sigh, and after some tossing on the futon, she was quiet.

This is my wife and Mitsuya's mother, the woman who will eventually look after my mother.

The breeze from the air conditioner gently caressed his forehead. Fumiya sighed quietly and opened his eyes to the dark. In theory, he was all for giving Mitsuya a sibling to honor his mother's wish. But making love to Reiko seemed a tiresome chore. Unless another incident could arouse his primal instinct and produce that brilliant red bead again, Fumiya would have to dutifully make love to his wife, imagining something entirely different all the while.

Wait a minute. The quickest solution would be for Reiko to bleed for him. If she were willing, Fumiya would no longer have to carry around a needle or live in fear of being caught again.

Now if only Reiko—

Listening to his wife sleeping soundly behind him, Fumiya began to imagine where she might bleed. He envisioned her distorting her face in pain, looking helplessly at the wound. The foot? Perhaps the hand, no, the arm. Would she cry out the way she had upon stepping on that needle? What path would the blood trace down her flesh? As Fumiya pictured himself licking the blood clean from her skin, a shiver rose up from the recesses of his body.

Oh, to see it again! If Reiko allowed him to glimpse even for a moment the blood flowing inside her body, Fumiya would carve that smell and taste into his memory, and then he would be able to love every inch of her red-blooded body.

He could never do it with Reiko's knowledge, of course. That much was clear. But it wasn't like he was going to prick her in public; she was his wife, after all. In that sense, what he was contemplating was far healthier and safer than continuing to stick needles on the train. Was there anyway to wound Reiko by accident? Couldn't she bleed in a way that might be forgotten in an hour?

Fumiya hardly slept that night, so desperately did he ache to watch Reiko being injured in some fashion, whether by stepping on another needle or a slip of a knife. If the outcome succeeded in satisfying his mother's wish of another grandchild and feeding his own vitality at the same time, he would have to see it through.

Eventually Fumiya abandoned carrying around a needle and spent several restless days anguishing over how exactly to orchestrate Reiko's accident. Stress mounted with every passing day, sapping what was left of the energy drained from the sweltering summer heat, but he could do nothing to relieve this obsession that gave him vitality.

One day, Fumiya returned after a rare night out drinking with a colleague to stave off the heat to find his younger brother there.

"This is a surprise," said Fumiya.

Kazuya sat next to their mother at the *kotatsu*. It had been a while since Fumiya had seen his brother, and he looked quite different. Their mother looked down, fighting back tears, and Reiko sat stiffly next to her, after coming to the door for Fumiya.

"Yeah, I guess." Next to several dishes of snacks on the table, his beer bottle sat half-full, yet Kazuya hiccoughed like he was already quite drunk. "I came by to ask you something."

As much as Fumiya wanted to get cleaned up after a long day, recognizing the menace in his brother's eyes, he changed quickly into a T-shirt and shorts and sat down at the table.

"Kazuya wants us to sell this house," said his mother, unable to stay silent any longer. Fumiya's eyes ricocheted between them.

"That's not what I want," said Kazuya. "I just figured that there was some part of the family assets coming to me, that's all."

"Assets? What are you—"

Reiko brought Fumiya a glass from the kitchen but any beer buzz he'd felt was long gone.

"I'm asking you to give me my share now."

"What's going on?"

Kazuya snorted and looked away in response. His mother explained that his business was failing. Fumiya peered timidly into his brother's face. Nothing frightened Fumiya more than the threat of losing his job and livelihood. Just the thought of his brother confronted with this very threat was enough to make him feel like he was being crushed.

"We expanded too much during the bubble economy, like everyone else. I guess you could say it came back to bite us in the ass." Kazuya, who had always been more enterprising than his older brother, had founded a small company with a few partners after graduating college. After some early success, they came to enjoy an extravagant lifestyle, buying high-end luxury condominiums and driving foreign cars. However, the business had become mired in debt the last few years and had declined to the point where they couldn't even pay employee bonuses. "I know you and mom hate giving out loans. So I'm just asking for my share." Kazuya had the ghastly look of a cornered beast.

But even Fumiya, who usually capitulated on everything, could not part with this house. "This house is all we have. Just what do you think is going to happen to mom if we sell the house?"

"You can do something about that, can't you?"

"You've got to be joking."

"Why the hell would I joke about something like this?!" Kazuya glared at him with bloodshot eyes and gnashed his teeth.

Stand firm, Fumiya told himself. *If I lose everything now, I won't have the strength to rebuild.* It was only because his father had left behind this tiny old house that he'd been able to scrape together a living.

"I'm begging you," pleaded Kazuya. "I've got nowhere else to go. This is sink or swim!"

"Kazuya, I can't. We've been planning to remodel the house next year or the year after—"

"Don't be so damn selfish! I've got a right to this house too!" Kazuya roar echoed in everyone's ears. He glared at Fumiya as if he would bite him. Reiko, sitting across from him, looked terrified.

"You're the one being selfish!" Fumiya shot back, undaunted, mustering all his courage.

Kazuya lunged with both arms and grabbed him ferociously by the chest. "Listen to me!"

"Stop it!"

"I'm desperate, damn it!"

Fumiya had managed to avoid any physical confrontation all of his life. As his brother's hands tightened around him, Fumiya's mind went blank with fear. He heard his mother and Reiko screaming, "Stop it!" "Papa, no!" Kazuya was surprisingly strong.

"I can't sell this house! I can't!"

"You want me to die in a ditch? I've got a wife and kid too!"

"You won't get your way on this!" shouted Fumiya, struggling to break free from under his brother. His arm swung an arc overhead.

Crash! As his hand wildly grabbed hold of the edge of the *kotatsu* table, he felt a sharp pain in his right palm. The energy drained out of his body. With Kazuya straddled over him, Fumiya, in a daze, brought the bloody hand up to his face.

"Oh, no! Papa!"

"Both of you, stop it!"

The glass was stuck deep in the palm of his hand. Crimson blood spurted out of the gash and dripped down the sparkling, jagged glass. The beer glass had broken and gouged into Fumiya's palm. Coming to his senses, Kazuya pulled away breathlessly, in shock.

My blood. My red...red blood. My Blood.

So intoxicated was Fumiya by its brilliance and beauty, he slowly got to his feet and turned his back on the others. The glass seemed to be stuck rather deeply. It glittered as the blood continued to drip from the fleshy part of the palm near his pinkie.

"Fumiya... I'm sorry—"

As soon as Kazuya spoke, Fumiya let out an animal cry that

he hardly recognized as his own. He folded his fingers over the glass into a fist and swung with all his might. Blood spattered in every direction. A sharp, throbbing pain shot straight up to his head as he buried his hand in Kazuya's cheek.

6

"You're brothers. Why did you punch him with glass stuck in your hand?" muttered the doctor, tending to Fumiya's hand under a bluish fluorescent light. Fumiya sat in a daze, his right hand given over to the doctor's care. He was still trying to remember what had happened right after the incident. But the moment he saw the blood streaming out of the wound, he'd lost all comprehension. *I'm alive, and my blood is red,* were the only thoughts left swirling in his head and he was overcome with a euphoria he'd never experienced before.

"There still might be some fragments. Hang on…"

His brother, who'd only suffered a bruised face, had brought him to the emergency room. Though he'd been told not to look, Fumiya couldn't help himself. He watched the doctor insert something resembling a long wire into his gaping wound. Although he'd been anesthetized, the right hand throbbed as the blood continued to spurt out. He felt something tiny being removed from the wound.

"Yeah, I see some fragments still in there. We'll need to wash the wound." The doctor started to give instructions to the nurse behind him.

With the tourniquet still wrapped around his upper arm, Fumiya gazed down at the cut. The crimson blood still flowed freely. The color was beautiful, chillingly bewitching. "What happens if you don't get all of them?"

"That could be dangerous. They might make their way into the blood vessels."

"What happens…if they do?"

The doctor looked at him curiously. "Let's see," he said, knitting his brows. "Well, glass is hard to pick up on x-rays, which is why it's such a pain. If it enters an artery, it might get stuck in a capillary. But if it enters a vein, it might end up in the lungs or heart." The nurse returned with a washbasin filled to the brim with clear fluid. "Sterile solution," explained the doctor. "I'm going to wash the wound in here. This might sting a little."

Fumiya quietly watched the doctor work on his hand. No matter how much anesthesia he was given, he could still feel the unpleasant sensation of being probed inside the skin. But that was nothing compared to the exquisite beauty of the blood.

"Don't trouble yourself looking for every last one."

"I beg your pardon?"

"A quick look is fine," said Fumiya, smiling weakly at the doctor. He recalled the story his mother told him as a child, the times he'd imagined the small needle racing through his body. Only this time, it was not a needle but a glittering shard of glass getting whisked along in the current of red fluid. The thought alone made him forget the pain and caused his chest to swell with delight.

"Well, we'll do the best we can, of course," answered the doctor, eying him strangely.

But Fumiya no longer heard him. It was then he realized: it was too troublesome to try and see someone else's blood. He'd only wanted to feel the blood coursing through his body, to feel the pulse of life in his own veins.

"It really is a pain once the glass gets stuck in there." The doctor continued to wash Fumiya's hand carefully in the solution.

Please, don't put in too much effort. Fumiya closed his eyes, praying for just one tiny piece of glass to remain undiscovered. He imagined the tiny fragment disappearing inside his flesh and making its way up his shoulder.

Fumiya wanted to make love to Reiko right that second.

WHORL

1

As Masao Akao waited for the light to turn at the crosswalk, he felt a raindrop land on his head. He reflexively looked upward where the sky was filled with dense gray clouds that looked ready to open up at any moment, but when he squinted at the shadows of the buildings nearby, there was no sign of rain.

"All these weddings one after the next... I can't stand it. Who would've thought that would be the drawback of working at an office with so many women."

Masao heard a melancholic sigh diagonally behind his shoulder. Turning around, he glanced at Kikuka pouting slightly, and smirked.

"You have to buy all these formal clothes that you can't wear everyday. Such a waste. Then there's the wedding gift money. It's all so depressing."

So depressing is what Kikuka said every time a college friend or co-worker got married. Masao knew that she wasn't complaining so much about the expense of having to buy a new outfit but about her anxiety at being left behind by so many of her friends rushing to the altar.

"I guess guys can get away with wearing the same suit," he answered. He pretended, as usual, not to notice the real cause of her bad mood, leery of how her irritation could often be directed at him: *How much longer are you going to neglect me? How long do you expect me to play bridesmaid to my girlfriends?* But Masao wasn't ready to settle down, so he continued to play dumb.

"Guys sure have it easy. You can wear the same clothes forever as long as you don't put on too much weight."

There she goes again. Just as he was beginning to resent having to go shopping when Kikuka was in one of her moods, he felt another raindrop on his head. *It's definitely starting to rain now.*

"You don't even have to wear makeup." Kikuka continued to pout, seeming not to notice the weather.

The light turned green, and the pedestrians started to walk across the street all at once. Despite the hustle and bustle of a weekend afternoon, the weather cast a dreary pall over the day, as a cold wind hinting of winter gusted between buildings. On a day like this, maybe it was better to do some shopping in the city than go for a long drive, thought Masao, recalling how Kikuka had called only last night to change their date plans.

"I was hoping to pick up an outfit after work, but you know how it is—you can never find what you're looking for in a rush. And besides, I could sure use someone's opinion. If I ask a friend from work, they'll know what I'll be wearing to the wedding, so I figured you were the best choice. That outfit you picked out for me last time was a big hit."

Having happily agreed to tag along, Masao found himself walking with Kikuka to the department store. There was nothing he hated more than going shopping with a girlfriend. As much as he recognized that generosity was an attractive quality to women, even the idea of having to trail after a woman like some well-heeled lapdog rankled him. But ever since he started dating Kikuka, he no longer found it much of a bother. She had a curious way of saying the magic words to string him along: *I just want to be with you, Masa.* Strangely enough, Masao didn't mind it one bit, perhaps because she was so good at playing sweet or because she valued his opinion so highly. *I'm so glad you came with me. You have such great taste.* It was refreshing, and above all, tickled his pride that Kikuka, who was a year older, depended on him as much as she did.

As they crossed to the other side, Kikuka looked up and held out her delicate white hands. "Oh, is it raining?" she said, her voice changing register.

A pedestrian in the crowd behind him echoed, "Rain," stirring the melancholy bug inside Masao.

"Rats, I didn't bring an umbrella," said Kikuka, furrowing her brows and looking around restlessly with her small, creaseless eyes.

Kikuka had a round face, dainty mouth, and eyes set far apart from her brows—an old-fashioned face out of a Heian era scroll painting. Masao thought this troubled look, as if she carried the weight of the world's worries, suited her better than a radiant smile. At the moment, that same face seemed to project the gloom inside his own heart.

Masao, trying to shake off his depression, said, "We're going inside anyway. If it's still raining when we're done, we can pick up a cheap plastic umbrella to keep us dry until the parking lot." He would have preferred parking in the department store lot, but it was terribly crowded and didn't want the irritation of sitting in traffic, so he'd parked the car in a garage opposite the train station.

Despite having remarked at the time that the extra distance would give them a chance to stroll through town, Kikuka now pouted and muttered, "Yeah...But buying a new umbrella would just be another wasteful purchase. You know how disposable umbrellas never get reused after that first time. Maybe it's better to buy a decent one."

Less than a year after they started dating, Masao came to learn that Kikuka was rather frugal. He was convinced that she would make a steady wife some day. "In that case I'll just buy a decent one," he offered. "I've been wanting to get a new folding umbrella anyway."

Kikuka smiled in relief, her small eyes narrowing into slits. She had cartoon-like features, etched just with simple lines. But it was this face and her diminutive size that he especially liked. She was easy on the eyes, and though her face didn't leave much of an impression, you didn't tire of it either. A face like hers was comforting and familiar.

As much as he'd grown accustomed to shopping with Kikuka, the women's department was still an unsettling place for Masao. The overly-friendly saleswoman modeling the store's fashions made unnecessary comments like, "Oh, you're with your boyfriend?" while solitary shoppers shot the couple icy looks. On occasion, he made eye contact with another man dutifully accompanying his girlfriend, which left them both a little embarrassed.

"What about this? Too plain?"

"Plain? Not at all. That style looks modest and refined."

"But how does it look on me?"

"I think the color brings out your white skin. Besides, you already have something in black and pink, right? But something in red or blue is too gaudy, not to mention it may go out of style in a few years. Gray is just too plain, but maybe brown isn't as common as you think."

After going around the floor and picking out several outfits, Kikuka began the usual dance of considering each item carefully. Though he was only rattling off whatever came into his head, Kikuka held up to herself the cocoa-brown moiré dress that Masao had originally picked out.

"Try it on," Masao suggested.

"I guess I will."

The saleswoman, waiting quietly behind them, cheerfully sprang into action. Masao took the purse from Kikuka's shoulder and tucked it under his arm, a routine that he'd gotten used to lately. Most of the saleswomen seeing this usually gave Masao a forced smile that was tinged with envy.

"Let me know when you're finished," said the saleswoman, closing the dressing room door behind Kikuka.

After Kikuka disappeared into the dressing room, Masao began to idly wander the store, clutching her purse. Browsing as he noted how expensive women's clothes were, suddenly he ran into his reflection in the mirror that was tilted slightly downward. Masao was able to see himself from an elevated vantage.

How bad is it? That melancholy feeling he'd barely managed to contain earlier was beginning to stir again.

Lately, he'd been sensing oncoming rain faster than others. More hairs in the shower drain after he'd rinse out the shampoo. Hairs on the pillow when he woke up in the morning. He'd tried to ignore what these things signified exactly, but now that he stood in the mirror, face to face with his own image, there was no denying it. He was going bald—and on the pate, to make matters worse.

Damn. This can't be happening.

Masao was only twenty seven. It was too soon, too cruel to have to worry about losing his hair now. In fact, it was precisely for that reason he'd ignored the changes. But under the dazzlingly bright lights of the department store, the contours of his head were clearly visible through his thinning hair. Sweat started to seep out of the pores around his forehead. Who would have guessed this fate? His father and father's father had plenty of hair. No, wait—there was the grandfather on his mother's side, who'd died when he was an infant. He was bald in his funeral portrait. *You've got to be kidding me. To think that this was the only thing he passed on to me.*

Just as Masao reached for his head, the dressing room door opened.

Kikuka emerged wearing the voluminous but simply cut brown dress. "How do I look?" she asked, preening anxiously in front of the mirror.

The saleswoman said, "Lovely," hurried off and returned with a lace shawl to match.

"You look nice," Masao said from behind.

Draping the shawl over her shoulders, Kikuka looked satisfied as she studied herself in the mirror and smiled at Masao. "I was worried it might look too plain, but I guess not."

"Not at all," said the saleswoman. "This color really doesn't work unless you're fair-skinned. And it looks perfect on you."

Flattered, Kikuka happily twisted her body left and right as if her earlier depression had evaporated, making the dress flare out with a slight swish of fabric.

How would she react if I went bald? Masao thought. Though she blamed him for keeping her single and working, what would she think if he were to lose all his hair and became prematurely bald? Would she still cling to his arm and introduce him to her friends? Would she still ask him to go shopping?

"I think I'll get this one. Masao?"

It was all he could do to nod at Kikuka, whose smile even looked more luminous in the new dress. As images of his balding head crowded unbidden into his mind, Masao left the store, glum and depressed, with a leaden heart.

2

Was the wind kicking up outside? A hard rain pounded against the blinds outside the window.

Kikuka sat on the bed, eyes glued to the television. "It's really starting to come down," she said, turning back her head in Masao's direction.

"Uh-huh," muttered Masao indifferently, his arms folded behind his head. Now that they were inside the hotel, he didn't much care how much it rained.

"If it rains on the day you buy a new outfit, it's also going to rain on the day you first wear it."

"What is that, an old wives' tale?"

"No, just the way it is for me. With shoes, too."

Kikuka, a worrywort, believed in odd jinxes and often read fortune-telling books. Knowing how angry she'd become were he to laugh and call such things stupid, Masao could only answer, "Oh." Besides, he could care less about Kikuka's troubles, given how he was nursing a funk of his own.

What do I do? If push came to shove, would I have to wear a toupee? You've got to be kidding me. Ugh. It was useless to worry about it now. He had no choice but to let nature take its course. At the same time, he felt there had to be something he could do.

"So I guess it's going to rain on her wedding day." Kikuka, wearing a hotel bathrobe, turned around and lay on her stomach next to him. "I hate the idea of my dress getting wet, but you know? I have to say I'm a little glad."

"About what?"

"The reception is going to be in a garden. *That's* a disaster in the making."

Masao turned and eyed Kikuka with fresh eyes. They'd worked up a good sweat, and the post-coital shower had washed away most of her make up, making her look childish. "Why would you be happy about your friend's wedding being ruined?"

Kikuka rolled over on her back and slid her body closer, her shampoo-scented hair spreading over the sheets. *Hair. What I would give to keep my hair,* Masao thought. "Well, it's not like we're all that close. We just happen to spend a lot of time together in the same office and because we started working at the same time. And to think, I bought a new dress and even a pair of shoes for her," Kikuka muttered. "She told me that she didn't have a boyfriend. That she wouldn't get married before thirty. It was all a lie. She completely caught me off guard." Kikuka's voice was angry, irritated. Soon the brunt of those feelings would be directed at him.

"Who's the guy?"

"I'm not sure exactly. A high school classmate or something." Kikuka turned over again and rested her head on Masao's shoulder. She stroked his bare chest quietly. Then Masao heard her sigh.

"What's wrong?" he asked.

"Nothing."

"You're sighing."

"I was just wondering...how long I'll be alone."

As soon as she uttered the words, Masao sat up and peered into her face. Kikuka met his gaze bearing down on her with eyes wide open. "You're not alone," he said. "We're always together."

"But I just don't see where this is going."

Brushing her hair away from her forehead, he was the one to sigh this time. All this talk of weddings. So many of Kikuka's friends had rushed to the altar since the start of the new year that she was shaken, and her irritation escalated with every new ceremony.

"You're your own person, aren't you? Just because you get married doesn't mean you'll find happiness."

"I know that. But still—" she said, looking down wearily, her lips trembling slightly.

It was a clear sign that she would burst into tears if he wasn't careful. Knowing Kikuka could turn on the waterworks on command when she wanted to and was quite capable of such theatrics, Masao pressed his lips to hers until the trembling stopped.

"I'm thinking about it, you know that," he whispered in her ear. "Stop worrying."

"Really?"

"Really." Masao kissed her longer this time. Her arms wrapped around his neck and gently began stroking his hair. "I'm trying to be responsible. I want to make you happy, so everything has to be just right."

"So what are you saying?"

"I'm saying you need to trust me."

Her bare legs tangled around his. Belying her appearance, Kikuka was always assertive in bed. Whether they went on a long car trip or shopping as in this case, she never refused him unless she had her period. In fact, it wasn't all that rare for Kikuka to suggest getting a hotel room.

"And if I trust you?"

"You're going to make me say it? Now?"

"Yes, now," she said, slightly breathless. But Masao was not about to utter the words she needed to hear. The truth was he wasn't ready to marry until at least thirty. It wasn't that he didn't like Kikuka; he just wanted to be unencumbered for a while longer.

Kikuka, who was turning twenty-eight this year, was always dropping hints that she wanted to have a baby before she turned thirty. Assuming he was the partner, he would become a father at twenty-nine. And if they were going to respect the proper order of marriage before children, Masao would have to marry her next year.

"Come on. *Now.*"

"Nope."

"Jackass. You never say it." Even as she looked away, she was already drifting into a certain mood. Masao knew that the most efficient way to recover her good mood, whether she was angry or sad, was to make love to her. Then she was cheerful again as if all her demons had been exorcised. Masao felt her hand tense. She tousled Masao's hair. "I love your hair. It's so soft, like a girl's."

A shiver ran up his spine, even though she had told him such countless times before. Kikuka had coarse, thick hair. How he envied her. Masao used to think nothing of how she loved to run her fingers through his hair, but now it was like she had put a knife to him.

What if I go bald? He considered asking her outright, but he feared he would never recover from the shock if she were to reject him. Even if she were to accept it, Masao himself would not be able to bear the indignity. He wasn't short and not at all bad looking, not to mention popular with the girls in the office. Balding? Surely, not him!

Even if I wanted to play the field a while longer, no one would give me the time of day. Even the prospect of marriage would become a pipe dream. Unacceptable! His intention wasn't to be a life-long bachelor; he simply didn't want to rush into marriage quite yet. Once he settled down, he intended to look after his family and to be a good husband and father. Maybe it was time to take the plunge now. It wasn't like he didn't have any prospects, after all.

Why, this woman in his arms would jump at his proposal if he asked.

"Oh, Masa..." Closing her eyes, Kikuka drifted into her own world. Masao regarded her face beaded with sweat and considered the possibility of living with this face for the rest of his life. He wasn't particularly adverse to the idea. He never grew tired of her, and the sex wasn't bad. Above all, Kikuka was reliable. She would make a good, steadfast wife.

"Masa?"

"Yeah?"

"Tell me that I can trust you. That we'll always be together."

"Always."

"Masa, Masa..." Kikuka twisted closer to him, her hands wrapping around his back. "I adore you, Masa. I'm crazy about you."

Whether Kikuka was aware of it or not, neither had said, "I love you" to the other yet. Masao planned to tell her when the possibility of marriage entered his mind. Should he tell her now? Would it be a prudent move to do so? As he thought about this and that, Masao desperately tried to arouse the feelings that were already threatening to wither away.

3

Masao felt something gently stroking his hair as he dozed. Even half-asleep, he knew it was Kikuka's fingers.

"You have a whorl here, too," she whispered, caressing the hairline around his forehead.

His eyes closed, Masao let out a noise that was somewhere between a snore and a proper response. Kikuka was a tough one, which was all fine and well, but Masao needed a rest to recover his energy. Although she was not exactly lustful, he grew nervous thinking about what his daily life might be like married to such a sexually aggressive woman.

"No wonder your hair is so wavy. How adorable," murmured Kikuka. When Masao rolled over on his side to escape her touch, she cried out disappointedly and immediately found the nape of his neck. "You have one here, too. I wonder how many whorls you have."

Masao had four whorls. One at the hairline on his forehead, the hairline at the nape of his neck, and two on top of his head. Though he'd never seen the two on his head himself, his parents and barber liked to remind him of their existence. They were why a crew cut was never a good look for him. When people with one whorl cut their hair short, the hair formed a shapely swirl, but for those with two or more, the hair swirled haphazardly in different directions, with gaps between the whorls. And when the hair was as fine as Masao's, the hair lay flat with no way to manage it.

"They look like eyes of storms, huh, Masa?" said Kikuka,

having regained her good humor.

Would he have to make love to her every time they fought if they married? The occasional date was fine, but his body wouldn't last if he had to perform every day. He might even grow tired of it.

Marriage, eh? Take the plunge, Masao! he told himself. Still, he couldn't make up his mind. Besides, he wasn't certain that he was actually going bald; maybe he only felt like he was. How wise would it be to decide the rest of his life so hastily? Perhaps he'd be better off consulting one of those hair specialists on TV instead. If a professional told him not to worry, then there was no need to rush into anything.

"Masa's whorls, spinning round and round and round..." Kikuka continued to amuse herself, prattling on and tracing the hairline on the nape of his neck. Meanwhile, Masao continued to work his mind, his eyes remaining stubbornly closed. He would give the hair specialist a call tomorrow. If they told him it was hopeless, he would tell Kikuka that he loved her.

Several days later, Masao worked up the courage to call the specialist, who told him, "How soon will you go bald? Well, that's always hard to say. That depends on the individual. Some people lose their hair in handfuls and before they know it, it's already too late." Masao was advised to come in for a consultation. Feeling very reluctant, he paid them a visit, but not before checking to see if anyone was watching him go in.

He was shown inside an all-white, sterile and brightly-lit room that at once resembled a clinic and a bright office, with potted pants and a television monitor in the corner. A promotional video played on the television. Masao wrote down his name and age on a medical form given to him at the reception desk and began answering the questionnaire:

Q1. Which of the following are your concerns? (Circle all that apply)
1. More hairs falling out
2. Hair getting finer
3. Dandruff
4. Scalp feels tighter
5. Generally thinning hair
6. Thinning hair in a particular area

Q2. Approximately when did you first notice the symptoms in Q1?
1. 1 month ago
2. 3 months ago
3. 6 months ago
4. Over a year ago

Q3. What do you think might be the cause of these symptoms?
1. Busier at work
2. Often wear hats and/or helmets
3. Side effect of taking prescription medication
4. Under increased stress
5. Nothing comes to mind

There were over 10 questions in all: do you smoke or drink regularly, how often do you shampoo your hair, do you use any hair products, etc. He answered the questionnaire, impressed that such wide-ranging questions were even necessary for a matter so minor as hair loss. He began to hold out hope that with this data, the specialist would be able to offer a solution that would make his problems go away. *It probably wasn't as easy as that...*

Once he filled out his medical information, there was nothing more to do but wait. Drawn in by the cheerful soundtrack, Masao eyed the television monitor, pathetically at first, until he found himself completely engrossed. A man, even younger-looking than Masao, nodded and listened to the doctor's explanation. A close up of the young man's head revealed that his pate was in a graver state than Masao's. The area around his whorl was already barren, the eye of the storm unfurling and spreading over the rest of the head. Next, he received a cranial massage, lying back in a reclining chair with one of those domed beauty parlor dryers over his head.

ACT NOW! DON'T GIVE UP! TAKE THE PLUNGE, CALL US!

Just as the man's dramatic transformation was about to be revealed, Masao heard his name called. A tiny man in a white coat stood, smiling broadly with a clipboard under his arm. "Thanks for waiting," he said. "This way please."

Masao was a little disappointed, having believed a young woman like in the commercials would attend to him, not the least of which, this man had a tantalizingly full head of hair. A glimpse of his thick mane alone instantly made Masao feel defeated.

After escorting Masao to the exam room, the man introduced himself as Kashiwagi, handed Masao a business card identifying him as chief counselor, and began to scan Masao's medical information. Standing up, the doctor said, "Excuse me," and combed his fingers through the delicate areas of Masao's head. "Yeah…" he muttered. "The whorl is pretty noticeable. Oh, hey, you have two whorls."

"Try four. On the forehead and the back of the neck."

"Wow," Kashiwagi let out, shooting a look at Masao for a second before examining the whorls himself.

"You have *four*. Now that's rare. Only 7% of people have a

double, you know. Less than 3% with three or more whorls. Isn't *that* something." Bewildered by why he'd be so pleased by such a thing, Masao cast a leery glance at the doctor, who resembled a peanut. Kashiwagi, perhaps sensing Masao's gaze, returned to his seat and smiled. "Let's work on trying not to lose those whorls."

"Lose?"

"As hair loss progresses, the whorls will eventually disappear. In your case, you're beginning to thin around the whorls on top of your head." After taking a deep breath, Kashiwagi leaned back in his chair and began to explain the balding process. The condition by which hair loss began not as a side effect of medication, but naturally, as in Masao's case, was called male-pattern baldness. While considered a disease, it was essentially a chronic condition with no natural cure. "The biggest cause is believed to be genetic, but it's an irregular gene, so no one's been able to isolate the exact hereditary components. It'd be nice when we do." Kashiwagi continued, "There are other factors such as strain on the skin, stress, and a shortage of oxygen going to the roots. Smoking and excessive drinking are also factors. Oh, I see here you don't smoke."

So it wasn't just his imagination. Masao was crushed by the reality that he was indeed going bald. He had to do something, to think about his future in more concrete terms. Would he be better off getting married before anyone noticed? Get engaged at least?

"So at this stage, the best we can do is to delay your hair loss. But we have seen some success with relieving stress on the scalp, improving blood flow through massage treatments, and cleaning the oil, dust and bacteria from the follicles so the roots are getting enough oxygen."

The doctor, looking Masao directly in the eye, spread out an ornate pamphlet. Despite the sales pitch that he knew was coming, Masao couldn't help staring down at the pamphlet.

The human head was said to have approximately 100,000 hairs. The life cycle of a male hair strand was two to five years; on average over one's lifetime, the growing period lasted four years, followed by a two- to three-week intermediate stage when the hair stopped growing, and then a two- to three-month resting stage between the hair falling out and a new strand growing in. Where a healthy head shed about sixty to seventy hairs a day, a head with male-pattern baldness shed hairs during the growth period due to an abnormality in the roots that impeded cell division. Gradually, the follicles were destroyed, preventing any more hairs from growing in.

"You know how balding men are said to have a higher sex drive? There's something to that because, as you know, testosterone is an enemy of hair."

Testosterone, the male sex hormone produced in the testicles and often found in muscle enhancement drugs, was known to cause hair roots to cease cell division. Recent research found that a substance called 5α-DHA, formed by the reduction of an enzyme called 5α-reductase, was responsible for inhibiting follicle cell division.

"We need to protect the roots from 5α-DHA. Strictly speaking, the hair loss would stop if the testicles were removed."

For a liberal arts-type like Masao, this was all difficult to wrap his head around. Furthermore, he had absolutely no intention of removing his family jewels.

"Now, let's see how your follicles are doing," said Kashiwagi, standing again.

No doubt the doctor would tell him that his follicles were dirty and launch into a lecture on the importance of hair care. Though Masao didn't necessarily think it a lost cause, he realized now that no amount of care was going to make his hair grow back and that preventing any more hair loss was the best he could hope for. It made him sad. *I'll have to keep coming here for the rest of my life, unless some revolutionary drug is invented, just to maintain the hair I have.* If the hair loss progressed, next came hair growth treatments and then a toupee. There was no silver lining to any of this.

"Yeah, your follicles are pretty clogged," said Kashiwagi."A bit greasy overall. You don't want your scalp too dry, but too greasy isn't good, either."

Exactly as Masao had predicted. *You have no idea how I feel!* thought Masao gloomily. *Yours looks greasier. And I don't wanna get lectured by some guy with a full head of hair!* Staring at the peanut-shaped doctor's head, Masao choked back his humiliation.

4

Masao felt refreshed after the follicle-cleansing treatment. Apparently, removing the dust, grease and bacteria not only saved the follicles from oxygen deprivation but made the nutrients in the hair restorer more likely to penetrate the roots. Kashiwagi had made a convincing argument for the treatments; even so, the regular visits would cost Masao dearly. In the end, Masao opted to forgo a membership and decided to buy the follicle-cleansing lotion and shampoo instead.

"But remember, your hair won't wait," Kashiwagi said in parting, smiling far more broadly than necessary. "You should seek professional help as soon as possible."

Better to prey on me once I'm beyond help, isn't that how you people turn a profit? But Masao couldn't act tough in front of the man who'd sussed out his weakness. After he was handed a pamphlet with an informational video, hair care handbook, a "special" membership form, and a product catalog in addition to his purchases, he said pleasantly, "Yes, all right."

A disease with no natural cure. Masao walked the darkened streets and replayed Kashiwagi's explanation in his mind. Premature baldness. An incurable disease. Even if there was no risk of pain or death, the weight of the word "disease" bore down on him, suddenly rendering him weak like an invalid.

A sick man has no future to look forward to. He caught himself looking at the heads of pedestrians passing by. Today, of all days, not a single chrome dome to be found. He spotted an elderly man with a healthy white mane, and let out a hopeless sigh. Masao's hair would not last to turn gray. Realizing this, he was seized with envy and jealousy.

He had to do something. As the doctor said, stress was hair's biggest enemy. What could he do to relieve himself of this stress? Try the follicle-cleansing treatments? Surrender immediately? Shave his head before anyone noticed? *No, the office would never allow it.*

Masao was a sales representative for a computer software company. Though the subsidiary company, bankrolled by a major corporation, had managed to produce modest profits even in this fallow economy, the office was not without rumors of layoffs. Only yesterday, he had turned a deaf ear to warnings that employees, from the top down, needed to stay current in order to remain relevant in this global cutting-edge industry. The company would not be pleased with a sales rep, not yet thirty, with an old-fashioned buzzcut. By thirty, he figured his baldness would've passed the point of no return.

What now?

At this point, he might have to seriously consider marrying Kikuka. At least then, he would be able to take his wedding pictures with a full head of hair. Having been roundly crushed by the events of the day, all Masao could do was go home to his studio apartment where no one waited for his return.

5

"In that case, I've got something you might want to try."

Two weeks had passed when Masao heard those benevolent words like a voice from heaven.

"It's still in the experimental stages, but I've been looking for someone like you." The once-in-a-lifetime words were uttered by Kanemitsu, an upperclassman from Masao's university days, who now worked in sales at a pharmaceutical company. He had called Masao out to plan a post-wedding party for a mutual college friend over a few drinks. For Masao, who'd become aloof and indifferent even around Kikuka, the reality that so many of his friends were getting married was a hard pill to swallow. But he could not refuse his senior's invitation. Plus, recently it had become almost customary for Masao to organize their friends' post-wedding bashes.

"But like I said, it's still in the experimental stages." Kanemitsu continued, "I can't guarantee that it will be 100% effective. But if everything checks out, this drug is going to be revolutionary."

Fortified by a few drinks, Masao began to confess his recent troubles, prompting Kanemitsu to mention a hair restoration pill that his company was developing. That was when he asked if Masao was willing to be a test subject.

"Really?" said Masao, leaning forward and staring earnestly at Kanemitsu.

"Why not?" Kanemitsu answered, smiling magnanimously before shifting a sober gaze to Masao's head. "I didn't think you'd have to worry over something like this. So is your old man or grandfather bald?"

"My grandfather on my mother's side."

"No kidding." Kanemitsu nodded deeply, and offered his condolences.

Then Masao confessed everything, about going to the hair specialist, being made to buy various hair care products, and being diagnosed with an incurable disease. As the pent-up words came tumbling out of Masao's mouth like water from a broken dam, Kanemitsu listened and nodded patiently, until finally he declared with a serious expression that the so-called specialist didn't have the latest research.

"Now listen, just because we don't know the genetic causes doesn't mean we can't treat it. The important thing is to improve the blood circulation in the scalp and give it the nutrients it needs. Then we tweak your hormone balance and you're good to go. We have the program already in place to make that happen."

Masao stared in awe, taken aback by how simple he made it all sound.

"Sure, it's important to keep the follicles clean. Cleanliness is important. But all those beauty products women lather on themselves? They aren't as effective as they think they are. The human skin acts like a protective layer, and while it may work well to expel certain things from the body, it doesn't absorb things as much. No matter how much you lather or rub on, the amount that gets absorbed into the body is miniscule. Nothing more than a temporary salve. Listen, whatever symptom you're trying to treat, if you're really after results, you have to treat it from the inside."

Kanemitsu was quite the silver-tongued salesman. Masao found his pitch to be much more tempting, more convincing than that of Dr. Peanut.

"So my company's been developing this pill that restores hair—"

"I'll do it!" shouted Masao. "I understand it's experimental.

Let me be a test subject, please."

Grinning happily, Kanemitsu nodded and explained how he'd already approached various staff members and doctors while making his sales rounds at the hospitals, so Masao would not be the only test subject. In fact, several people had already started taking the pill, even though he hadn't even started data collection yet. Masao leaned forward even more.

"If you're really interested, I can get you the pills in the next two to three days. Two weeks' worth, initially. And then another two weeks' worth, if you don't experience any weird side effects. You should start seeing results after two months. You just have to answer a couple of questions every time you get a new batch."

"How much is this all going to cost?"

"Like I've been saying, you'd be participating in a clinical trial. We're the ones that have to pay *you*."

What music to his ears! What a stroke of unexpected luck this would be if this pill could make his problems go away. Masao had hardly touched any alcohol recently, after hearing that heavy drinking accelerated hair loss, but on this night, he drank to his heart's content. "A *senpai* is the best thing to have in the whole wide world!" Masao repeated, keeping Kanemitsu at the bar despite indicating he'd like to get home soon.

"This has been really bothering you, hasn't it?" muttered Kanemitsu. Even his slightly mocking tone sounded pleasant to Masao's ears.

In order to take the yet-to-be-named hair restoration drug, Masao was asked to sign an agreement stating that the test subject could terminate use if the pill did not achieve desired results or in the off-chance it caused side effects. If the side effects persisted after terminating use, however, compensation would only be nominal, and the company would not be liable for claims against the drug.

"Don't worry, this is just a formality," said Kanemitsu.

Masao trusted his *senpai's* smile and reassurances. He received his first round of the wonder drug, realizing he would get to see Kanemitsu every two weeks to get more medicine.

This has to work. Please.

Apparently, hair grew at a rate of 0.3 to 0.5 millimeters a day. Though new hairs would be readily seen on the barren region of the head, they had to grow at least 5 to 6 centimeters before they were visible among existing hairs, even if one used a mirror to inspect the new growth. Masao would have to wait at least two weeks before he would see any visible results. Not to mention, there was no telling when the pills would take effect on the dormant follicles. Staring expectantly at the very ordinary capsules, he resolved to stick with the regimen for at least two months.

Autumn had slipped by without notice. Masao and Kikuka went for a drive one wintry weekend when she asked, "Is something going on with you recently?"

"What do you mean?" said Masao, noting the bare trees along the road as he drove.

"I don't know, you seem a little different since we last met."

Though the couple spoke often on the phone, between friends' weddings, memorial services, and various other things that came up, they had not seen each other in weeks. The couple rarely went out on weeknights because overtime at work seldom allowed him to keep a date. Kikuka was busy with cooking and English conversation classes, and they preferred not to rush through dinner to go to a hotel, which was almost always the final destination in Kikuka's mind.

"Nothing's going on," answered Masao casually, gripping the steering wheel. Sensing her gaze, he glanced at Kikuka sitting in the passenger seat.

"Something I sensed on the phone, too."

"Like what?"

"You seemed upset just until recently, but I felt bad about asking, so I held back. And today, you seem to be in a better mood." Kikuka had a sixth sense for these things. Perhaps emboldened by her various obsessions with fortune-telling and jinxes, she had a habit of looking strangely confident about intuiting such changes. "Something's up."

He couldn't possibly tell her that he'd been worried about going bald. Kanemitsu had also told him that his involvement in the clinical trial was to remain confidential, so Masao made up an excuse off the cuff about having tough times at work.

"At work?"

"Yeah, all sorts of things just came up. But everything is fine now. Actually, I'm glad we had the time apart, because I might have taken it out on you."

Kikuka listened intently to Masao's story, then gave a nod. "That bad…?"

"Yeah, I've been a bundle of stress lately, and with all the year-end parties coming up, it's damn near exhausting."

A frigid wind gusted in from the window that was open just a crack. A stretch of various types of trees beginning to lose their fall foliage came into view. Masao gazed at the bleak landscape, the frail, outstretched branches of the trees resembling withered arms, and recalled the top of his head. Come spring, these trees will sprout new leaves, turning this place into a thick forest. Yes, brought back to life, rustling their leaves in the wind.

By spring… As desperate as he was to check each day, he had abstained from looking in the mirror, worried that he might discover either no new growth, or even that his hair loss was getting progressively worse instead. Three weeks had passed since he started taking the pills. Though he'd decided to check for signs of growth in the mirror after exactly a month had passed, Masao fantasized about his dramatic transformation daily.

"Oh, I'm so sorry to hear that," mumbled Kikuka.

A woman like this might not come along so often, thought Masao, touched by her concern. Kikuka was not beautiful, but she wasn't exactly a troll, either, not to mention reliable and caring. No doubt she was a good cook, attending all those cooking classes. She was from a solid family, and her father was a man of reasonable standing. Kikuka would make an ideal wife. *Maybe I'll ask her to wait until I'm thirty.*

With a reasonable explanation, Kikuka would probably wait for him. After all, she was the one that desired marriage more than he did. He would propose it to her once they settled in at the hotel tonight. If a verbal promise wasn't enough to satisfy her, he would offer to meet her parents as evidence of his commitment. Get engaged, if necessary.

Having thought through his options, Masao felt a sense of relief come over him. Certainly there was no telling what might happen, as with any relationship, but when he considered that the pills might not prove effective, proposing to Kikuka was like taking out an insurance policy.

6

Then, the unthinkable happened. As soon as the couple went up to their hotel room and Masao took Kikuka in his arms and kissed her deeply, he realized that his body was not responding. *This can't be happening*, he thought, in a panic. *This never happens to me.*

"I've missed you, Masa. I've been so lonely," she cooed, pressing her body against his. "Finally, we're together." Normally Masao would ease Kikuka back onto the bed and peel off her clothes one by one as he kissed her. Then it was her turn. Kikuka would unbutton his shirt, slide her hands down to his belt, and undo his trousers until she squealed like a child who'd found her toy. But at this rate, he couldn't let her take off his pants.

"You haven't been cheating on me, have you?" whispered Kikuka, unusually sensuous, her eyes already glistening.

Masao panicked, his mind not comprehending what had happened to his body. *This isn't like me. Most mornings, I wake up with—wait a minute.* Come to think of it, he might have been soft down there on recent mornings.

"Oh, Masa…" Kikuka was waiting with rapt attention for him to ease her onto the bed and fall on top of her.

Cold sweat seeped out of the whorls on top of Masao's head. He had to act as if everything was totally fine, but his mind was in a swirl. *What do I do? What's happening? What's wrong with me?*

Sweat beaded on his brow. He pushed her down on the mattress and took more time than usual kissing every inch of her body, caressing the small of her back, waist and down her buttocks, until Kikuka moaned. All he could do was stall for time.

Kikuka twisted inside her clothes, as if unable to wait any longer. But Masao's body did not respond. Something was clearly not right. It wasn't that he wasn't in the mood; he wanted to seize Kikuka this instant, yet his body refused.

"How about a hot bath?" Masao said, pulling away. "It was pretty cold out. I don't want you catching a chill." Masao untangled himself from Kikuka's arms and got up. Kikuka lay on the bed and stared sullenly at him like a puppy that had been told to wait. "I'll go run the water, all right?"

As Masao walked to the bathroom desperately feigning calm, he was overcome with dizziness. He turned the faucet, letting the water fill the tub, and went into the washroom.

Dropping his trousers and briefs and sitting on the toilet, Masao quietly peered down below. Nothing.

Were he alone, he'd want to scream, to pummel the wall and shout, *What the hell is going on? Why is this happening to me?*

He could hear the water running from the other side of the door. The bathtub was enormous; no doubt Kikuka would want to take a bath together. But he couldn't possibly, not in his present condition, not at the risk of hurting Kikuka's feelings, to say nothing of shredding his own pride to pieces.

There was a soft knock at the door. "Masa? Is anything wrong?"

His eyes jumped toward the door. Masao swallowed hard. *Damn it, there had to be some way out of this fix.* Never had he been this frantic for an escape in his life. Even when he tried to pass off a lie or avoid blame as a child, he had never been this wild-eyed with panic.

"Masa? Are you all right?"

To hell with "all right." Try pissed off. Panic-stricken. Miserable. He felt like crying. Letting out a whimper, he pulled up his trousers. After flushing the toilet, he opened the door and found Kikuka standing there, frowning and tilting her head slightly.

"My stomach started hurting..." said Masao, squeezing the words out of his parched throat.

"You're sweating! Are you in much pain? Do you have an upset stomach?"

Masao went out into the bedroom and sat at the edge of the mattress, rubbing his stomach gingerly. He had no choice but to fake an illness. There was no way he could please her sexually in his present state.

"Was it something you had for lunch? Did the pain come on suddenly?" Kikuka now looked at him worriedly and stood before him.

Glimpsing her small breasts in his eyeline, he wanted to tear off her blouse and press his cheeks against the swell of her chest. "I don't know, my stomach's been feeling funny—oh, would you mind checking on the bath?"

Kikuka turned heel and pattered to the bathroom. When the water stopped, silence filled the bedroom with the tropical island-inspired motif. "What should we do?" Kikuka said, returning. "Do you want to go to the hospital?"

"No, maybe if I just lie down for a little bit."

Nodding deeply, Kikuka diligently removed the covers from the bed, the figure of innocent bravery. With a hand resting on his stomach, Masao lay on his side and curled into a ball to seem as sickly as possible.

"Should I call down for some medicine?"

"I doubt they'll have anything decent at a place like this. Maybe my stomach will settle down if I rest a little," he muttered slowly. Masao closed his eyes, since it was too painful to look at Kikuka any longer.

"I don't understand it. This has never happened before." Hearing Kikuka's voice behind him, he felt the bedsprings give a little as she lay down beside him. She began to stroke his hair. "Maybe it's the stress from work."

"..."

"I think that's it. Look, you're even beginning to lose some hair."

Masao felt like he'd been punched in the back of the head. His entire body tensed and his stomach began to churn as if his phantom pain might suddenly become reality.

"Poor baby, are things that bad at work?"

Kikuka's tone remained calm and peaceful, yet Masao detected more pity than what was called for. No longer able to lie there, knowing her eyes were trained on the back of his head, he sat up. Kikuka looked up in surpirse.

"This isn't working. Sorry, I'd better go home."

"But how are you going to drive?"

"I'll be fine if I'm careful. Staying here isn't doing me any good."

Disappointment and worry came across her face. Unable to look her in the eyes, Masao mumbled, "Sorry," and hastily put his outfit back together.

"Do you want me to drive?"

"Can you?"

"I've driven my father's car sometimes, so I should be fine if I don't go too fast."

"Yeah, okay."

Masao said nothing more afterward. Not only did sitting in the passenger seat of his own car make him uneasy, with Kikuka's driving to worry about in addition to his sudden physical dysfunction plus his premature baldness, there was no earthly way he could carry on a normal conversation. Believing his silence to be caused by stomach pains, Kikuka refrained from her usual idle talk out of consideration for him. Never had Masa experienced a date as awkward or as dull as this.

"I hope you feel better. Call me, okay?" Kikuka said wistfully in parting, after Masao dissuaded her from following him inside to nurse him back to health. He wanted to be alone. No, he needed to be alone so he could try to calmly assess the reality that had befallen him. Just what the hell did he do to deserve such a fate? He wasn't so much miserable as angry. *So this is what it means to be thrown in a pit of despair,* he thought.

A week later, the morning of the day Masao would meet Kanemitsu after work, he examined his hair for the first time. Still smarting from Kikuka's innocent quip at the hotel, he peered into the bathroom mirror, forbidding himself any high expectations. Just as he'd feared. No change. In fact, the crown of his head appeared to be getting thinner, the hairs looking sparse enough to count, like the trees in the forest he'd seen during their drive. And to add insult to injury, he was no longer functioning below the waist. Masao was convinced: Regardless of how much he tried or woke up every morning desperate for change, he couldn't get married in his present condition.

"It's only been a month. You're going to have to give it at least two," Kanemitsu said that night, handing Masao another two weeks' worth of pills. He then told Masao about a test subject who'd finally begun to detect some peach fuzz in his sixth week of use. Having been bald for over twenty years, the man had cried tears of joy. Masao let out an envious sigh. "He's also been getting regular scalp massages and follicle-cleansing treatments. You still keeping up with that?"

Masao nodded slowly. "Has anyone in the trial experienced any side effects?"

"Not that I've heard," answered Kanemitsu. "Why, are you having any side effects? Better you tell me sooner than later."

Masao nodded, saying nothing. He had suspected the hair restoration pills were causing his erectile dysfunction, in which case, it was likely that other tests subjects had also gone limp in that area. But in light of how no one had reported any side effects, to say nothing of the man who'd reported actual hair growth, there had to be another cause. Had he obsessed too much over his baldness? Would he have to get his hands on some Viagra?

"Anyway, let's wait and see a while longer."

After being sent off by words that were neither entreaty nor encouragement, Masao found himself utterly alone. He considered going to a phone sex or hostess club but decided against it."It" would be useless anyway.

After the year-end party season came Christmas. Ever since his narrow escape from the hotel, Masao had avoided seeing Kikuka, citing one excuse after the next, knowing how suspicious she would get if they met without their usual hotel stop. But there was no escaping Christmas. Even Masao was well aware of the romantic dreams that women envisioned for this day. *I can't fake an illness this time.*

His depression worsened by the day. The more he put on a cheerful front at work, the more tired and depressed he grew when alone. He found himself brusque with Kikuka when she called, but as much as he regretted it, there was nothing Masao could do. He knew he had to do something but didn't have the slightest idea what. As he toiled away at work as a diversion, before he knew it, Christmas had crept up on him.

"You've been so busy, are you sure?" Kikuka said on the phone the night of the 23rd. He assured her that although Christmas Eve wouldn't work, Christmas Day was fine since it fell on a Friday. "All the hotels are probably booked, though," he added timidly, as a preemptive measure.

"You're probably right," Kikuka answered, rather unexpectedly. "Besides, my father would find out that I have a boyfriend if I don't come home that night."

That Kikuka came from a strict, traditional family was usually cause for complaint, but in this case Masao was relieved that he might be able to end the year without incident. He would be able to figure out his next move over the New Year's holiday.

On Christmas Day, low clouds had loomed over much of the morning. The weather reports had forecasted the possibility of a White Christmas in the Kanto region. Masao had spent his lunch hour buying a designer ring. It was not intended as an engagement ring, but an urgent attempt to keep stringing Kikuka along for a while longer, a tacit and uncomplicated way of conveying to her that his feeling for her had not changed.

Kikuka arrived at the appointed place in her work clothes, making her appear more mature and dependable than usual. After they were seated at the restaurant that Kikuka had chosen and reserved, the couple toasted the night with champagne. The restaurant was mood lit by oil lamps on the dining tables, while music box renditions of Christmas songs played in the background. Lovers were brimming over with happiness, intoxicated by the well-orchestrated ambiance with little regard for what the holiday truly signified.

"Sorry about last time," began Masao. "I went to sleep and woke up completely fine the next morning, like it was all a dream." Then he began to talk about his day, about the everyday trifles he'd usually tell her over the phone. Observing how patiently Kikuka listened, unusually chic in her black turtleneck and gold necklace, Masao thought, *She's too good a woman to let go.* If she really wanted, he wouldn't mind getting married next year.

"Listen—"

"I was thinking—"

They spoke up at the same time, running into each other's words. Kikuka looked surprised. Masao smiled and tilted his chin in her direction. "Go ahead."

Pursing her already-dainty lips, Kikuka looked him in the eye resolutely and said, "I don't think we should see each other after tonight."

Masao stared at her delicate face, his right hand gripping the small box in his pants pocket. He had been ready to give her the ring just then. What was she trying to tell him now?

"I went on an arranged introduction, for marriage." Sighing quietly, she began to talk quietly about how the proposal of a lifetime had come by way of her father's acquaintance. How her parents were ecstatic about the proposed marriage. How the dismal economy plus the increasing number of women quitting after marriage were making it hard for her to keep working. How she desperately wanted to become a mother before she turned thirty. How her potential marriage partner seemed awfully taken with her and how she didn't think him all that bad, either. How astrological readings revealed that they were a perfect match. In short, the marriage negotiations were progressing very smoothly.

"But you're going out with me," Masao blurted out, dispassionately.

For the first time that night, a smile came across Kikuka's face—a peaceful and gentle yet adamant smile that would give in to nothing. "You don't really want to get married, do you? I know you don't like me all that much."

"That's not—"

"It's true, I know it. You don't think I've noticed you avoiding me lately?"

No, you've got it completely wrong. It isn't that I've been avoiding you! Masao fumbled for the words to explain, as Kikuka continued, smiling, "If we go on seeing each other like this, I might start blaming you. Always questioning why, my unhappiness growing by the day. I was hoping if we end it here, we could just say goodbye amicably."

Masao knew that had no right to try to stop her. Even if he dissuaded her from walking out on him now, it was only a matter of time before she found out about his dysfunction. He was no longer qualified to be the husband of a woman who wanted children as soon as possible. Masao fell silent, unable to do little else but wonder if he'd ever faced a harsher reality. After Kikuka suggested they at least finish dinner, Masao shoveled down the meal that suddenly tasted like mud and sucked back the champagne. Excessive drinking accelerates balding? At this point, Masao couldn't give a damn.

He emptied the bottle of champagne and a bottle of red wine himself and by the time he stood up to go, his world was spinning.

"Are you okay?" asked Kikuka tenderly, despite having just ended their relationship.

Shaking off her hand, he settled the bill and stumbled outside. A chilly wind blew. The worst Christmas of his life was coming to a close. Then he felt a drop on his head.

"Rain..." he muttered, squinting up at the night, but he was too drunk for his eyes to focus properly to see the fine drizzle falling from the sky.

"Are you sure?" said Kikuka, glancing up. "Oh, you're right," she said after a pause. "I felt a drop on my face."

Masao grimaced. He was balding and impotent and to top it all off, freshly dumped by this woman. They headed for the train station together. Kikuka put an arm through his to stop him from drifting in a diagonal line. He felt miserable, fighting back tears.

"You know, " Kikuka said, when the subway station came into view. "There's this drug I heard about that you can get in America..."

" ... "

"It's supposed to work wonders for restoring hair." Just as he tried to tell her that he'd already started taking such pills, Kikuka continued, "But the moment you stop taking them, you'll go back

119

to losing your hair again, so you're really not supposed to take them for extended periods. Only for special occasions."

When they came upon the subway entrance, Kikuka let go of Masao's arm. Unlike her collected demeanor of earlier, Kikuka's lips quivered as if she might start to cry.

"Maybe you should try cutting your hair shorter. Longer hair makes the thinning areas stand out more. You know, because of your whorls."

With these parting words, Kikuka said farewell and pattered down the stairs. He watched her go, dumbfounded that the woman whom he'd believed he would eventually dump had just dumped him. The rain turned into snow. Couples walking past rejoicing. Standing there at the station entrance, vulnerable to the frigid wind, Masao allowed the snowflakes to fall on his head, his face.

Masao had no idea how he'd found his way home. By the time he staggered into his apartment, he was drenched from head to toe. Though he'd sobered up considerably, he stumbled over countless things strewn about the floor on his way to the answering machine. He had hoped to hear a message from Kikuka, but what he heard was Kanemitsu's voice:

"Listen, I need you to stop taking those pills. I'll explain in depth later, but there's been some unexpected side effects. I don't know—something to do with a hormonal imbalance causing impotence in some of the test users. You need to stop taking them. You'll be fine once you stop. Sorry. I'll call you later."

Merry Christmas, Kanemitsu's voice hoarsely echoed. In the window, blackened by the thick of night, was Masao's reflection, sopping wet with only the crown of his head shining like a nimbus.

BUTTOCKS

1

Hiroe heard her name called by her homeroom teacher in the final period before school ended. The teacher was tall, skinny and helpless looking, wore thick glasses and had perpetual bed head. Usually his face was a blank, making it nearly impossible to tell what he was thinking or what kind of mood he was in.

"Come to the front," the teacher said in a rough voice that contrasted with his appearance. For a brief moment, Hiroe flashed back to what had happened during lunch. As usual, Hiroe and her two partners in crime had harassed Emiko and tried to get her to give them her wallet. And as usual, Emiko had cried, "No!" which acted like a signal for the other girls to yank her hair, kick her in the torso and butt and twist her arm outwards until she cried uncle. Hiroe wondered if Emiko had ratted them out to the homeroom teacher.

"I can't bring it in anymore. No way. My parents will find out," Emiko had said in a quivering voice in the science class prep room, her eyebrows furrowed as she chewed on her lip. For the most part, Hiroe simply looked on as her comrades did the dirty work. They acted as her subordinates, truly convenient "best friends" for the past year.

"That's got nothing to do with us, you moron," one of her friends said with a smirk and poked Emiko in the face. Hiroe wasn't hard up for cash, but she knew that taking the girl's money would get her in the most trouble. Most of the money stolen would be used by her friends to buy alcohol.

A snowy scene sprawled outside the windows like a brand new

sheet of drawing paper. In recent years snowfall had been scarce, but ever since January there had been an increase in snowy days and everything outside had turned into an expressionless, illusionary world of white. Sometimes sunlight would shine through the clouds and turn everything into glittering silver, but for the most part gray clouds crowded the skies. Falling snow impeded Hiroe's field of vision, making it hard to judge distances. This empty scenery bored and irritated her.

"You know what's in this room, don't you?" Hiroe whispered, slowly pointing to the shelves lined with chemicals, as Emiko continued to gnaw at her lip and sat on the cold floor. "Hydrochloric acid, even sulphuric acid. Get it?" Emiko looked thoroughly spooked and stopped breathing. Hiroe and her friends guffawed and shoved Emiko around until the bell rang for class.

There wasn't much time left until junior high graduation. The desire to choke the life out of Emiko was what had united Hiroe's posse. There was no real reason. It was just something that came about when Emiko joined their class in 9th grade.

Emiko stood out. When it was time to choose a class rep, work in groups or respond to the teacher's questions she would always be overly cheerful, her voice too merry, too lively. She always seemed to be having too much fun, no matter what she was doing. That's what got on Hiroe's nerves. In fact, it might have been nice to have her as a friend. But Hiroe wanted to limit her circle of friends to girls who were similar to her and easy to get along with. That was the way she wanted things that year, the years previous, even in grade school.

"Koide, did you hear?" The teacher's face was pockmarked with acne scars. He was apparently still under 30, and occasionally he'd show up with fresh scabs from careless shaving which only added to his unclean appearance. As the teacher stared at her with his small eyes enlarged by his glasses, Hiroe made a decision: If she were asked in front of the entire class about what happened to Emiko, she would feign ignorance about everything. After class, she would exact thorough revenge.

However, the words that came out of the teacher's mouth were wholly unexpected. "Congratulations," he said. As Hiroe stood there dumbfounded, he turned to the rest of the class. "Koide has been accepted to a girls' high school in Tokyo." There was a commotion in the classroom. "Everyone, give her a round of applause!" Sporadic claps rang out in response to the teacher's order. For a moment, Hiroe didn't know what kind of face she should make. She'd forgotten that today was the day that school acceptances would be announced. And besides, hadn't her mother asked her teacher to keep the fact that she'd taken the entrance exam a secret from her classmates? If she was rejected she'd be humiliated, and her parents didn't want her to be the target of rumors or ridicule. But the teacher smiled for the first time as if he'd read her mind and figured, "You were accepted, so there's no need to hide it anymore, right?"

"The hell? You never even said you were applying to a Tokyo school," said one of the boys.

"Figures. Her daddy is the famous Dr. Koide, OB/GYN!"

"Moving to Tokyo for high school? So jealous."

As her classmates jeered, the teacher told her to say something. *You traitor. Blabbermouth. I don't wanna say anything. It must be a lie. Why was I accepted?* But the teacher who never so much as made a pun wouldn't pick a time like this to make a joke.

"Come on, Koide. You're the first student to get accepted someplace," the teacher pressed, his expression unchanged. Hiroe had no choice but to turn and face the class. Smiles. Blank faces. Bafflement. Envy. Curiosity. Amongst all those faces was Emiko's. Her expression was one of unmistakable relief. Once she saw her, Hiroe took a deep breath and smiled her usual smile.

"Sorry to keep it a secret, but that's how it is. If you ever come to Tokyo I'll show you around. I'll be back for summer vacation, so please don't be strangers."

"Hey, what kinda school is it? What's it called?" asked the class gossip, leaning forward. Hiroe said it was a high school affiliated with a well-known all-girls college.

"Oh! I've heard of it! I know that school!" shouted another girl. "It's a real top-notch place!" she exclaimed, her eyes widening. The rest of the class made a noise like a sigh and her friends wore expressions that were a mixture admiration and despondency.

"Wow! So you can just slide into that college without taking any exams?"

"That school must be totally different from private schools around here."

"Hiroe, you were studying hard in secret this whole time, eh?"

Hiroe made a face as if to say, "Isn't that obvious?" But she still felt that this shouldn't be happening. Her parents were enthusiastic, but she didn't really want to go to that school, and figured she wasn't competent enough to get in anyways. Of course, she wanted to go to Tokyo someday, but she figured it'd be fine if she went after college. She wanted to finish high school where she could commute from home, a public school where she and her friends could all attend together. That would be much more fun and cozy. And besides, there was Tatsuro. They had promised each other that they would go to the same high school.

"Everyone, do your best." After a nod from the teacher, Hiroe walked slowly back to her seat.

"Hey Hiroe, that's pretty cold," said one her friends. They had surrounded her immediately after school let out.

"You were absent last week. You weren't sick, you were in Tokyo!"

"You could've at least told us." The girls would usually gather after class to bully Emiko, but now they faced Hiroe with subdued

126

expressions, looking to one another for confirmation and sighing. Hiroe couldn't work up the nerve to apologize and simply continued to pout. She hadn't planned on getting accepted, so she hadn't thought she was lying to her friends and hadn't expected them to come down on her like this.

"You said we'd all go to the same high school but that wasn't your real intention, was it?"

"No, you're wrong," she retorted, but it was obvious that wasn't enough to wipe away the doubtfulness that clouded their eyes. "Anyways, let's walk home together," she said, wanting to smooth things over. "Let's go downtown and grab some burgers before heading home. I'm on clean-up duty today, so can you wait for me?"

Her friends exchanged glances and shook their heads, still looking displeased. "We gotta study for entrance exams. We can't just laze about like someone who's already gotten into a school."

"You acted all cool and collected so we let ourselves slack off, too, but we can't do that anymore."

"You really pulled a fast one on us."

The two girls hurried away. "What the hell," Hiroe muttered. "Hmf." Even her fellow classmates on clean-up duty all made vaguely unpleasant faces and turned away. No one said a word to her. Hiroe suddenly felt that she was forced to stand apart from everyone else. An unexpected sense of loneliness spread through her.

Why was I accepted?

This shouldn't be happening. Once released from the hell of entrance exams, she should have been able to clasp hands and celebrate with Tatsuro and her friends. As Hiroe trudged through the snowy streets towards home she wondered if she really had to go to Tokyo. *There must be something I could do to stay here. And how am I going to explain this to Tatsuro? How can I ever convince him?* She sighed heavy white breaths that dissipated in the cold air.

"Get ready. We're going to Tokyo tomorrow," her mother said after congratulating Hiroe as soon as she got home. "You're gonna be really busy," her mother continued, looking very pleased. The family's clinic next door was still accepting patients, but her father, grandfather and uncle took turns coming over to the main building to give their congratulations. Her grandmother who lived further away hurried over with a gift envelope full of money. Hiroe was increasingly perplexed.

"Did I really get in?" Hiroe asked. Her mother was in high spirits making arrangements for the next day.

"Of course," said her father with a smile.

"That's why we're going straight to Tokyo tomorrow. I've already booked a hotel. The one from before. You liked that place, right?"

"But it's still so early. I don't have to go all the way to Tokyo just to fill out school forms—"

"What are you saying? It's not just about forms. You also need to get fitted for a new uniform and apply for housing. I'll even take you shopping for new stuff. I already told your school that you'd be absent. Besides, we don't need them to keep this confidential anymore," her mother said peremptorily. She padded partway up the stairs in her slippers, then stopped and turned around. "We're throwing a party for you tonight and your grandfather and daddy's associates will all be there, so be sure to greet them properly."

"Are we flying tomorrow?" Hiroe asked instead of responding.

"It looks like snow tomorrow. A train would be better. But if there are flights tomorrow we can take a plane instead."

"I don't wanna take the train. But we really don't have to rush, do we?"

"We do," her mother said resolutely and continued up the

stairs. "Oh, I have to get deliveries from the sushi and meat markets," she said, and scurried back downstairs. "Ah, the florist, too. Oh, I'm so busy." Hiroe watched her mother dash through the living room, thinking her mother was acting as if she herself had gotten into the school.

Tokyo, huh?

She didn't hate the idea of being in a city where it never snowed. *I could go shopping wearing normal shoes, walking on dry ground.* Even so, she still didn't feel enthused. *What will I tell Tatsuro? How can I explain it?* Hiroe went up the stairs, coming to the conclusion that there was no point in trying to make excuses. She couldn't think of what to say on the phone. Apologizing wouldn't change the situation. In the end, she was different from everyone else. She had to follow a suitable path as the only daughter of the head of the Koide Obstetrical Hospital. That's what her mother had often said.

2

It wasn't until a week later, on the night before they were scheduled to return to their snowy hometown from Tokyo, that her mother told her she hadn't been accepted solely of the basis of academic achievement. They had gone to the new school, filled out paperwork for the private dorm she'd move into in April, ordered new bedding and household goods from a department store and scheduled them to be delivered as soon as her room was vacant, went shopping in Harajuku, went to the movies, and Hiroe had finally come around to the idea of starting a new life in Tokyo come spring when her mother had decided to tell her the truth.

For an entire week, her mother had taken her shopping so often that her mood brightened every chance she had to whip out her husband's credit card. They had gotten quite comfy in their hotel room. Her mother took a sip of the wine she'd ordered from room service and said earnestly, "You understand, don't you? You see that this is evidence of how seriously we're thinking about your future, right?" In other words, they'd bribed the school into taking her on. The dean of the school happened to be an acquaintance of her father's and allowed her to sneak in. Hiroe found herself at a loss for how to react. Should she be angry? But it was too late. Her mother had spent a shocking amount of money on her that week, and above all, she'd finally started to look forward to moving to Tokyo.

"Do you understand why I'm telling you this?"

Hiroe shook her head weakly. She figured her mother was going to tell her to behave and work hard, as it probably cost a lot of money to get her accepted, but couldn't bring herself to say as much. It was too humiliating to put into words.

Her mother tipped the glass of blood-red wine to her lips and took a tiny sip, sighed quietly and turned to face her daughter. "Don't worry about the money. Your father and I would do anything for your sake. But come spring, you'll be on your own. You can't get lazy or spend all your time goofing off just because there'll be no one around to keep you in line. If your grades don't improve, we won't be able to cover for you."

"You mean I'll become a drop-out?"

Her mother sighed sadly. "You might be a little behind everyone else at the start. Just don't forget that there's nothing I can do if you don't work hard at keeping up those grades." If she didn't, she could get kicked out of high school before graduation. Her parents had gone to the trouble of getting her in the backdoor, and even if she was near the bottom of her class, as long as she graduated she could just ride the escalator up into the affiliated college. "So even just a little bit more effort is fine, but you gotta study hard," her mother said with a serious look on her face. "Listen, if you're forced to switch to a different school all our relatives will find out and the neighbors will start talking. That will damage your future prospects."

And they'd end up with mud on their faces. But her mother had a point. If Hiroe had to drop out, all her classmates who had looked at her with envy, even the betrayed Tatsuro, would double over with laughter. *Serves you right!* they'd point and laugh. That alone was an unpleasant thought.

"I'm not going to tell you to spend every waking moment with your nose in a book. I just don't want you to forget that this is not the time to be slacking off or playing around. You can have fun, but there are limits when you're just a high schooler."

Hiroe toyed with the silver pendant her mother had bought

her in Ginza a few days prior and found she had no choice but to nod meekly. After climbing into bed, she still turned things over idly in her mind. She was freed from having to take any more entrance exams and could move to Tokyo, but she had to shoulder that much more pressure. She didn't really understand why she had to work that hard. She wanted someone to tell her, "There's no reason to push yourself so hard. You can be as you are. You can go to a high school in your hometown." If only Tatsuro would say as much to her. But even that dream was short-lived. She could hear her mother's even breathing as she slept in the bed next to her's.

They landed in their grayed out hometown that was covered with heavy clouds, a world that was unimaginable under the dry, windswept skies of Tokyo. Even still, Hiroe loved that town. It was a quiet, calm, settled place on the shores of the Sea of Japan. She didn't want to leave her friends and family that lived there.

The next day, she headed back to school for the first time in a while, breathing out white vapor and wanting to savor the crunch of snow underfoot. As the front entrance came into view, she ran into Tatsuro who was wearing a scarf over his mouth and navy blue snow boots. *Ah!* she thought, smiling reflexively. But as soon as he saw her, he looked away quickly and walked right past her.

He's angry.

Hiroe nearly crumpled with sadness. She'd missed him terribly all week and at the very least wanted to hear his voice, but now he made it clear that he wanted to avoid her. "Horii!" she said, sounding forced and formal. She always made a point to call him by his last name except when they were alone, even though they'd been in the same class since 8th grade. Tatsuro turned around slowly, still bent slightly forward at the waist. Hiroe ran to him, kicking up snow. Other students passed them by. The snow absorbed the sound of their voices, so once the other kids moved slightly away they shouldn't be able to overhear their conversation.

"I've been wanting to call you," Hiroe said quietly.

"Hmf," Tatsuro grunted, facing away.

"What? I was away. Just got back yesterday—"

"I know. Tokyo, right? You're going to some girls' school there."

"So you've heard." The rumor had spread. That was practically a given, since a week had already gone by. Tatsuro didn't respond as he started walking again towards the school. As she watched his cold figure walk away, instead of feeling sad, a small flame of anger flickered inside her. "What the hell? If you knew, then you should say 'congrats!'"

Tatsuro pivoted. "I'm not in any place to congratulate anyone! I've still got exams ahead of me! I'm trying to get into a prefectural school!" His voice was loud enough to be heard by other students walking by. She noticed her classmates looking at her with a mixture of surprise and indifference, with smirks on their lips. The wind was knocked out of her and she stood there in a daze. Tatsuro faded into the distance as the snow blotted out his figure. Her fate had drastically changed. She might never speak to Tatsuro again.

I'll throw them all away. This town, these 'friends.' I'll be the one to end it.

The rest of her schooldays until graduation were as dull as sawdust. On top of exam season starting in earnest, a vicious flu spread through the school, resulting in almost no days where everyone was present—sometimes over half the student population was absent at once. Mixed in with the students who would graduate to employment and others who were relegated to private local high schools as they weren't good enough to get into the top public schools, Hiroe made use of the study periods and was drafted to help out with the class yearbook.

It was a blessing to be busy with things outside of regular

classes. Her "best friends" had long since abandoned her, and other classmates formed new cliques based on which schools they would attend, so Hiroe was very much friendless.

Graduation day finally came. The snow hadn't yet melted away, but the sunlight spilling through the clouds was a harbinger of spring. Aside from one student who was moving to a slightly larger town within the prefecture for a job, Hiroe was the only one leaving town. Her homeroom teacher sent her a sheet of heavy colored paper that her classmates had signed.

"Have fun in Tokyo!"

"Let's hang out during summer vacation!"

"I'll be going to Tokyo for fun, so please show me around!"

"Your future is bright!"

"Please be my friend, even if you become a big-shot!"

Hiroe looked at the paper that the teacher she'd never really warmed to and her 34 classmates had signed and burst into tears. She felt sorry for herself because even though they all wrote such sweet messages, there was no one she could confide in, no one she could tell, "I don't want to go to Tokyo."

3

Hiroe moved into a girls' dorm not far from Shibuya that was managed by a privately-held company. There were dorms at the school, but her mother disapproved of the fact that there were no single rooms and the facilities were generally old, so she'd found this one instead. Fifty girls from across the country lived in the dorm that resembled a typical apartment building.

After the school entrance ceremony ended and her real mother waved goodbye, her dorm mother stopped by her 100-square-foot room that would serve as her stronghold in the city with a copy of the dorm rules. "Just pretend you've suddenly gained a whole bunch of sisters. You can talk to us about anything, so you can take it easy here. These rules might seem like a pain in the neck, but it's really just a list of obvious things. If you just go about your daily routine, this place shouldn't feel all that formal, but of course it's going to be a little different from living at home where you could do as you pleased." The dorm mother was too young to be called elderly, yet she was clearly older than her mother, perhaps around 50 years old. "But," she said, peering into Hiroe's room, "you've certainly made yourself at home already." Hiroe followed the woman's gaze. The dorm room had come with a desk, a bed and a small closet already installed. In addition, Hiroe and her mother had purchased rugs, a small dresser, bookshelves, a low table, cushions, a floor lamp, and an alarm clock. Everything was brand-new.

"Oh, we already have a vacuum cleaner you can use," the dorm mother shrugged as her gaze stopped on the small vacuum standing in the corner. Indeed, Hiroe knew there were cleaning tools available for everyone to use. But her mother had said, "You don't want to clean your own room with a vacuum that's sucked up dirt from other people's rooms, do you?" and bought a new one, despite the fact that Hiroe had never even vacuumed at home.

"Well, I guess that means you'll keep this room spic and span. I'll introduce you to your dormmates at dinner. Well, only about a third of the girls are here yet. The rest you'll meet as you settle in," the woman said and walked away in a hurry. Hiroe didn't think she'd ever like the dorm mother. She sighed, alone once again, sat on her bed and stared absently at the paper with the guidelines.

- Avoid disturbing others. Please be aware of other residents when using the baths, washroom, toilets, washing machines, rec room and other communal areas.
- Curfew: 8 p.m. for high school students; 11 p.m. for college students. Please report any overnight stays outside the dorm by 3 p.m. the same day.
- Breakfast is served from 7 a.m. to 8:30 a.m. Dinner is served from 6:30 p.m. to 8 p.m. You must prepare any other meals yourself. If you use the kitchen, please turn off all heating implements and clean up after use.
- Please only use the baths between 4 p.m. and 11 p.m. You may use the showers 24 hours a day.
- You are personally responsible for any valuables. You may leave large amounts of cash with the manager. Please lock your door when you leave your room. You are responsible for keeping track of your keys.
- You may use the rec room at any time. However, please keep the volume of the TV low and conversations quiet during late-night hours.

- If you have television sets, stereos or other electronic entertainment devices, please keep the volume low and turn everything off before you leave your room.
- As a general rule, any persons who are not residents of this dorm are not permitted inside. Men are strictly prohibited.
- You are responsible for picking up your dry cleaning from the manager's office.
- Please direct any questions to the dorm mother or to senior residents of the dorm.

There seemed to be an excessive number of rules. But there was no mention of how they were supposed to get up in the morning. *Is there a way to ask for a wake-up call like they do in hotels? But there's no phone in my room. Wait, are we supposed to get up on our own?* Hiroe had never been a morning person. Her mother usually had to call to her at least three times before she could haul herself out of bed. That's the way things had been for as long as she could remember. Yet now she lived away from her parents, and starting tomorrow she would have to get out of bed, bathe and dress herself and get to school all by herself. On top of that, she had to study hard or she'd end up a drop-out with no place to go but home where she'd cause her parents to lose face.

All she could do was sigh and roll over on her bed. *Starting today, this is my room. This is where I belong.* But just one step outside her room put her in an unknown world filled with strangers going to and fro. Even lying on her bed she could hear soft noises, the sounds of strangers going about their lives. There was nothing to do about it. In time, she'd get used to it. She would have to. She took a deep breath and got up from her bed and decided to clean up around her desk. Her new textbooks lined her desk menacingly.

Thus her Tokyo days began. For Hiroe, who started out and

continued to be nervous during those days she felt less that everything was fresh and new, and more that everything was happening in an alternate dimension. She was taken aback by the fact that her classmates all wore trendy, sleek clothes. Without a single male student to be seen, the school was filled with lively voices as gorgeous, lovely girls (who seemed so grown-up one could scarcely imagine they had only just graduated from junior high) spoke lucidly and unabashedly. There were cliques who had been together since their years at the affiliate junior high and walked around as if they owned the place. Hiroe felt threatened by the way they talked, their belongings, their behavior. She had been one of the most fashionable and stylish girls in her junior high and stood out as the daughter of a doctor, yet that pride she'd cultivated didn't pass muster here. After all, she was a country bumpkin with a provincial accent, and since she knew nothing about city life she couldn't keep up with their conversations. Such a realization dealt Hiroe a hard blow.

"Koide lives in the dorms?"

That wasn't to say she had no friends who talked to her, but she was so nervous she couldn't respond properly. Her face turned bright red when the teacher called her name and her tongue tied itself in knots.

At this rate I'll be left behind, I'll be the only one who can't move forward.

Besides, she hadn't gotten into the school on legitimate merits. She shouldn't even have been allowed to wear the same uniform as everyone else. Such thoughts terrified her. Naturally, Hiroe was isolated and spent her days running between her dorm room and school. Her dorm, at least, was a place where she belonged. After a while of seeing other dorm residents, some of them would talk to her.

"Welcome back!"

The ones who spoke to her were older residents, the dorm mother or the manager. They'd ask her if she'd settled in at school, how she was faring. That alone was a saving grace. Yet she could never call this environment that was to utterly different from home "comfortable." Besides, the age range of the dorm residents was too broad. Hiroe was the only high school sophomore. There were three juniors and two seniors, and the rest of the 40-odd residents were college or grad school students. The three juniors all went to the same school and did everything together. The two high school seniors went to different schools. One was a bookworm, and the other wore makeup like an adult and spent most nights outside the dorm.

Then there were the women, college age and above, whose backgrounds and areas of study Hiroe was wholly unaware of, who seemed to exist in a separate world. Some women dressed gaudily and wore shockingly heavy makeup. Others were curt and gloomy, and changed their outfits and makeup so often Hiroe had a hard time remembering their faces. Those women had habits, mannerisms and expressions she'd never witnessed before in members of her gender, even among her schoolmates in junior high, her mother, grandmother, aunts or other relatives.

There was one woman who would hog the prepaid card-operated public phone for hours. Another would set up camp in front of the TV any chance she got and ate junk food. Some girls would come back to the dorm to change their outfits several times a day, while others almost always wore the same clothes and hardly ever went out. Others still seemed to want to remove any trace of their existence, taking meals alone and rarely leaving their own rooms once inside the dorm.

The most depressing thing for Hiroe were the communal washroom and toilets. Depending on the day, some mornings the washroom was jam-packed. Even though they all had posters in their rooms reminding them to keep the toilets clean, sometimes they were filthy, with tampons and pads strewn about.

Above all, Hiroe hated taking baths. The bathtub itself was wide, clean and brightly lit, but it was nearly impossible to enjoy it in solitude. If she went in alone thinking she had it to herself that day, someone else would come in shortly thereafter. If she picked the wrong time, a number of girls would all bathe together, their shrill voices ricocheting around the tile-covered bathroom, and Hiroe wouldn't know what to do with herself.

"So then what?"

"So then my boyfriend says, 'Fuck you' or somethin' and the other guy said 'No, fuck *you*' and kicked his ass."

"You gotta stop going out with guys like that."

"Oh, did you hear? What's-her-name says her period's late."

"Ugh, they're totally doing it."

Everyone would sit around without a shred of embarrassment, shaving or doing exercises in the buff while trading gossip. At worst, the girls would talk frankly about sex and, upon noticing Hiroe's presence, would laugh and say, "Hope you're taking notes."

Hiroe had bathed with her friends when they went on school trips and had gone into hot springs with her mother and grandmother before, but she wanted to be able to bathe alone, where she wouldn't be disturbed by anyone or have to worry about others' gazes.

She called her mother almost every night on her new cell phone. When she voiced her worries her mother said, "Well it can't be helped, it's a communal bath," sounding wholly unconcerned. "You just don't have much experience with such things, so you're unused to it. But listen, you can't just take showers. You need to warm up by soaking in the bath. Okay? I can't fly down and take care of you if you catch cold."

Even without her mother's warning, Hiroe had never used

the showers. Even if she'd wanted to, they always seemed to be in use, and the one time one was available she'd peered inside and saw a nauseating amount of long hair all over the basin.

"I want to go home."

"Don't say such a thing now. We're lonely without you here, but we put up with it because it's the best choice for your future. You can come back in May during the long holiday, okay? I'll send you an airplane ticket."

Hiroe had finally worked up the courage to tell her mother how she really felt, yet her mother barely paid attention. All she could do was say good night and hang up the phone. Each day felt impossibly long. She could hardly wait for the vacation in May, each moment lasting an eternity. On the last day of classes before the holiday, she left school and went straight to the airport, arriving in her hometown still wearing her school uniform.

"You look well!"

"Your skin looks so white! You've gotten prettier!"

Her mother and grandmother picked her up at the airport and smiled happily when they saw her. They complimented her on how great she looked in her uniform. They jumped to the conclusion that she had shown up in her uniform because she wanted to show it off. When they arrived home, her father and grandfather were thrilled to see her in uniform and wanted to hear all about Tokyo. For the first time in a while, Hiroe was surrounded by family and was the center of attention. She talked about things at school and life at the dorm. She didn't know why, but she only spoke of funny or amusing things that had happened.

"Glad to see you've been having fun," her father said with a smile. Hiroe had promised her mother that she would pretend she still thought she'd gotten accepted to the school by her own achievements when she was around her father. If she let on that she knew, it would sadden him. He didn't give the school a large donation in order to make her feel obligated to him, and he never wished to make her lose her self-confidence. Her mother told her that her father would be totally happy as long as she kept her grades up and fully enjoyed life as a student.

"Aren't you glad you went to Tokyo?"

"Of course. If I want to go to college in Tokyo I should get used to living there anyways, and there are girls from all over Japan in the dorms, so it's really interesting."

How am I able to say such things so easily even though I don't mean any of it? Yet everyone in her family, including her father, seemed to take her at her word. When they took note of her weight loss, she said she was on a diet and they all laughed.

One day during the break there was a class reunion. Back before graduation, Hiroe and her classmates had decided to get together and trade stories about their new lives. Hiroe wore clothes she'd picked up in Tokyo and headed towards her alma mater, walking through the town that was readily embracing the coming verdant season.

"Wow, you seem totally different."

"Yeah, it's like you're a Tokyoite now."

Her former classmates stared at her curiously. However, Emiko, the girl she had bullied as if it was her *raison d'etre*, and the girls she had once believed to be her best friends now kept their distance, never bothering to talk to her in a friendly manner. In fact, despite their relentless teasing, Emiko was now friends with her two former pawns. All three of them had gotten into the prefectural high school that Hiroe had wanted to go to.

Our paths are different. I'm different from these kids who got stuck in the sticks, Hiroe earnestly repeated to herself. Although she missed them so dearly she could cry, she plastered a smile on her face that felt so frozen and rigid that it may as well have been made of ceramic.

"What? Emiko, you already have a boyfriend?" came a voice that pulled her out of her reverie. By reflex she looked to where the voice had come. There sat Emiko, her face reddened as she punched her loud-mouthed friend bashfully in the arm.

"Who is it?" asked someone, leaning in.

"Someone everyone knows."

"What? Someone from our school?"

Until just a few months ago, her two best friends had chirped at her elbows like two songbirds. Now they flanked Emiko, giggling as they confirmed their classmates' suspicions. Hiroe heard the name "Horii."

Tatsuro.

Tatsuro's face flickered in her mind. Tatsuro's cold, blank face as he turned away from her that wintry day, his figure erased by the falling snow. Up until then, he had been kind, occasionally smiling at her shyly. He had liked her first. That's what she'd heard, anyways.

And now he's with Emiko. Fine. You all can just stay here, huddled together in your tiny little world. I'll become a real Tokyoite. I'll become someone that's very hard for anyone to get close to. Hiroe bit her lip, thrust out her chin and sucked back her lukewarm juice.

4

Things started to get strange around the beginning of June. After the long vacation, Hiroe had returned to Tokyo determined to get more comfortable with her new lifestyle. As a result of her redoubled effort she began to make some new friends. It was around the time that the results of the midterm exams were posted, and she was relieved to see that her grades were only slightly lower than average.

Every time she had a bowel movement, she felt a sharp pain in her rectum. She'd had trouble with constipation ever since moving to Tokyo and thought the pain was due to overstraining. Yet she only managed to defecate once every few days and the pain made her anxious and the prospect of having to use the bathroom made her depressed. Besides, she hesitated at staying in the bathroom for too long. She couldn't take her time if she worried about someone waiting outside or anticipated a knock at the door.

Why does it hurt so much?

Even when she managed a bowel movement, it cause a sharp pain that seemed to get worse as time went on. Hiroe panicked when one day she saw bright red blood on the toilet paper. *Blood? When I'm not on my period? And from my butt? It must be the toilet paper.*

Her family had had bidet toilets for several years which allowed her to clean up with warm water. She had never had a bowel movement at school during junior high. Even if she felt the urge, she held it until she made it home. Yet now she was forced to use poor-quality toilet paper. Surely it was the toilet paper that was having a terrible effect on her body. She was able to forget the pain after five or ten minutes, so she didn't think there was anything wrong. But the terrible pain would be back every few days.

That day, she had strained until her sweat had run cold and finally managed to void after a week's interval. "So? Anything interesting happen today?" her mother asked on the phone. Hiroe responded, "Not much."

This constipation can't be good. I'll have to buy some new laxatives. The efficacy of the medicine that she was taking waned the longer she took it.

"You always say that." Her mother sounded slightly disappointed. Ever since she was little, Hiroe had hidden important things from her family, knowing that telling them would only cause a huge ruckus. Issues at school, with her friends, about herself—her mother didn't know any of it.

"Well, I'm just going about my business all day long."

"Oh? Well you're certainly feeling fine if you can take such a saucy tone with me," her mother giggled. Hiroe was envious of her mother's peacefulness. Hiroe said she was about to take a bath and hung up. Since the toilets didn't have bidets, her only option was to clean up in the baths.

There were three girls already in the baths when she arrived. One was Mutsumi Tamaki, a student at an all-girls college who was more friendly than most. She gave a thin smile to Hiroe as she walked along the cold tile floor. Mutsumi was soaking in a tub with her brown hair pinned back in a clip.

Hiroe rinsed herself off and got in the tub. She was too embarrassed to look Mutsumi in the eye, so she sat facing the same direction.

"Hey," Mutsumi said calmly. "I noticed this a while back, but..."

"What?"

"You've got a pretty big ass."

Hiroe, gobsmacked, glanced sideways at Mustumi, who in turn stared fixedly at her manicure. "It's massive," she practically sang in a carefree tone.

"Oh, really?"

"You don't think so? It's big compared to your upper body. That's why you look like a duck when you wear jeans." Mutsumi jumped up in the tub, the displaced water splashing Hiroe, the older girl's rear end appearing before her eyes. "Small asses are in style. Childbearing hips are out. Why not try and lose some weight?" Mutsumi's voice pinged around the room. Hiroe stared at her body as she walked out. Tan lines from the summer before still marked her adult female body. Her bottom was unexpectedly small. Her waist was trim and her hips were curvaceous, yet her butt was indeed tiny.

"I was thinking about buying that exercise thing they advertise on TV," Hiroe said in a lull in her dormmates' conversation.

"Oh, that thing that's like walking on air? I wonder if it even works."

"But it's bulky, it'll take up space."

"Then let's have everyone pitch in to buy one and keep it in the rec room so we can all use it."

"But what'll the dorm mother say?"

"If we're all in agreement, who cares? She's just an employee, she's not in a position to shoot us down."

"Right, right."

As she listened to her dormmates chattering in the baths, Hiroe slowly reach back and touched her butt as she soaked in the tub.

A duck? It's not that big. And on top of that I have to deal with that awful pain... My butt.

Hiroe hadn't ever been concerned about her body until then. Her breasts were visible to anyone who cast their eyes downward, and being aware of their glances made her realize that she was growing up. But her skin was fair, her limbs of average length, and while she didn't think her face was anything to brag about, she was confident that when made up she was prettier than most college-age girls. She had never thought that she should be worried over her looks. To think that her butt was as big as a duck's.

The baths were filled with the sound of laughter. Hiroe thought they were all ridiculing her and was seized with the desire to disappear. Just then, she saw a yellow rubber ducky that someone had brought in sitting on the edge of the bathtub. She found herself unable to look away from its behind.

From that day on, Hiroe stared at the bottoms of everyone around her at the dorm and at school. She scrutinized her classmates' bodies when they were in gym clothes, as their figures were usually obscured under school uniforms. In their navy blue shorts, she could see that indeed most of the high school girls had small asses. Since everyone had small behinds, she had assumed that hers was the same, but apparently that wasn't the case.

In her room, she would close the curtains and stand naked in front of her dresser, turning sideways and twisting around in order to look at the lower half of her body from every possible angle.

I gotta do something. At this rate I'll be different from everyone else. They'll laugh and call me "ducky." I'll be the only girl who doesn't look good in the sleek, polished clothes that everyone in the city wears. And why are there two butt cheeks anyways? Why are they so fleshy? I have a bad butt. These two lumps of flesh around my painful anus are bad. They're just hunks of fat. Why can't I just chop them off?

Part of the problem might have been the constipation. Her intestines were sucking up too many calories from what she ate, which turned into extra fat that was then stored around her hips. She knew what she had to do. She would cut back on fatty foods and get herself a small butt.

Diet.

She had rarely heard that word in junior high, yet as soon as she entered high school she'd heard it several times a day from classmates and dormmates alike. She had always thought dieting was for other people, but now she needed to go on one herself.

That day, Hiroe made surreptitious changes to her life. She listened intently whenever anyone around her talked about dieting. She learned that the most effective method was purging. For example, girls that she had gotten friendly with would dash off to the bathroom immediately after eating ice cream or burgers while on an after-school shopping trip in Harajuku or Shibuya to force themselves to vomit. If you eat, you gain weight. But it's hard to override the temptation of food, so you eat as much as you want then throw it up before any of it gets digested. That explanation was very easy for Hiroe to understand.

Sticking several fingers down her throat and forcing herself to throw up was challenging at first as it was painful enough to bring tears to her eyes, but within a few days she got used to it. In the evenings, she ate dinner as usual and then went to throw up. She didn't have time to make herself sick in the mornings so she skipped breakfast. School lunches became Hiroe's only source of nutrition. She continued to take laxatives. While the rectal pain never went away, the laxatives helped soften her bowels which lessened the intensity of the pain somewhat.

Hiroe's grades for her final exams at the semester's end were a little higher than her results for the midterms. Her mother arrived in town for parent-teacher conferences and after discussing Hiroe's progress with her teacher fairly danced with joy. As a reward, she bought Hiroe a designer watch. Hiroe fastened the brand-new watch around her wrist and headed home for summer vacation.

"Have you lost weight?" her father asked after seeing her for the first time in a while and furrowing his brows.

"Mom said the same thing, but my weight hasn't changed. I've been exercising, though." Hiroe strove to keep her expression composed.

Her father looked oddly awkward and simply said, "Exercise, eh?"

"She's getting to be that age when girls start thinking about polishing their stuff," her grandmother joked.

"You haven't got tapeworm or something, do ya?" her grandfather chimed in and the whole family laughed together around the dining table. But Hiroe's uncle noticed the red spots on the back of her hand. After sticking her fingers down her throat several times a day, raw marks had formed where her front teeth grazed her knuckles.

"What happened? Did you burn yourself?" he asked, looking at her hand as she held her chopsticks.

"No," Hiroe answered, her face composed. "I always get so sleepy when I study so I press a ruler or pencil into my hand. I guess it left a mark."

"You stay up studying even when you're that tired?"

"You really are enthusiastic, aren't you?"

Her family sounded surprised. Hiroe smiled proudly, as if to say that was all very obvious.

"People really can change, eh?"

"I was afraid you'd turn into one of those brassy high schoolers they show on TV, but I guess my worries were unfounded."

"I'm a daughter of the Koide clan. I'm not that stupid. Studying is actually pretty interesting if you understand it."

At that moment, Hiroe recalled that she used to hate these kinds of dinners with her whole family. They were annoying, noisy, forced and affected. She hated that her family normally led disparate lives, only to gather for some special occasion and act all chummy. Until they had gone full-tilt when it came to getting Hiroe into high school, her parents had been totally indifferent to her. They had only put effort to get her into that school because they wanted to shore up their chances of nabbing a decent son-in-law who could take over the hospital when her father retired. It was for their sakes, not hers.

Why had I forgotten that?

She realized that she had allowed herself to get caught up in their scheme. She had put up some resistance by not bothering to study for the entrance exam, but they had been able to twist her arm with their purse strings.

It all seemed so stupid. She felt like there wasn't a single thing she had done of her own free will. The only thing left that she could control was her own body.

"Thanks for the meal." Hiroe quickly put down her chopsticks. Her family simply smiled pleasantly at her. "I'm a bit tired so I'm going up to my room."

"Oh, so soon? Get some rest, then."

"Good night," they all said as she left the living room. She walked up the stairs and went straight into the bathroom.

5

Someone was being very noisy outside. Hiroe cracked open the door of the shower stall. The commotion instantly died down as her eyes met those of a very startled girl.

"Oh, I am so sorry." The girl, who looked to be older than Hiroe, turned around all aflutter and told the two adults waiting behind her, "Not this way, that way." She hurried past the adults who carried two large bags each and beckoned them to follow. She must have been a new student moving into the dorm that spring, and those were probably her parents.

So plump. So uncool.

Watching the girl's rear end as she hustled away, Hiroe wanted to laugh in scorn. *Chubby girls shouldn't wear jeans. They just make your ass look fat.*

That day was the final Sunday of March. The number of new students moving into vacant dorm rooms was at its peak. The new semester would start next weekend. Hiroe walked past the bathroom, washroom and laundry room and went up the stairs just as two new girls came running down the steps. They seemed to be high schoolers. They, too, seemed startled when they saw Hiroe and stood rooted to the spot.

"Hello," Hiroe said, smiling deliberately. *Be nice to the new kids. Greet them with positivity.* So read the poster hanging in the rec room since last week. The girls' mouthed the word "Hello" in return. Hiroe walked past them, a smile still on her lips.

"What the hell was that?" came a whisper as Hiroe turned around on the landing. She stopped and listened intently.

"Was that a skeleton that just said hello?"

"What's up with her? Is she sick?"

"I wonder how old she is."

The girls' voices faded away. Hiroe, seized again with the desire to laugh haughtily, continued up the stairs.

Say whatever you want, little piggies. Calling people skeletons? How rude. If you're going to call me anything, call me "slender."

As soon as Hiroe got back to her room on the third floor she peered into her dresser mirror. She saw a girlish face looking back, with pale, translucent skin and large, ephemeral eyes. Her hair was brown and thinning a bit, but it looked lighter than when she had tons of jet-black hair. The bridge of her nose was more defined and prominent than before. Hiroe slathered a good amount of lotion onto her face. The backs of her hands were sinewy, which bothered her somewhat, but she thought that was still better than having thick, fleshy hands. Her arms were very thin. Everything looked very stylish on her, and her arms moved in a supple, soft manner, like those of a ballerina she saw once on TV. Hiroe had been fascinated by the ballerina as she gently undulated her arms like the wings of a bird.

Full-blown results of her efforts began to show up as autumn began. She threw up whatever she ate and started taking enemas on top of continuous use of large amounts of laxatives which resulted in her losing an amusing amount of weight. All her clothes looked baggy on her. Thanks to the enemas, her body felt totally clean and clear and the pain and bleeding from her anus lessened. Since she was eating far less, her bowels were smaller. Hiroe believed that if she stopped having bowel movements altogether, her problems would be solved. *Stop eating to avoid having to go to the bathroom. Stop eating and any excess fat will melt away naturally.* Simple, clear logic.

"Have you lost weight?" came the chorus of voices at school

and in the dorm. Hiroe saw envy in her friends' eyes. Some friends would ask what kind of diet she was on, her current weight, her measurements, and for the first time since moving to Tokyo Hiroe felt a sense of superiority over those around her. Just like when she was in junior high, she had confidence and composure and felt comfortable talking to anyone.

Clothes shopping became fun. She had always gone shopping with her mother, but now, for the first time, she was able to experience the joy of going out on the town and peeking into boutiques and thrift shops to find cute, cheap clothing.

They'll never be able to call me "ducky" again.

Hiroe became even more obsessed with losing weight. The marks on the back of her hand turned into tough, dark callouses which stood out so much that some accused her of purging, so she started wearing a handkerchief wrapped around her hand.

Towards the middle of autumn, she stopped menstruating. Low blood pressure caused her to faint during gym class. When she noticed everyone staring as the male gym teacher carried her to the nurse's office, she felt like a princess in a fairy tale.

Hiroe sat staring off into space one day when there was a knock at the door and the dorm mother poked her head inside and stared intently at her. "Your mother is here to see you."

"I don't want to see her," Hiroe said, repeating what she had said the day before. This exchange had gone on every day for a week. Usually the dorm mother would just sigh and say, "Guess it can't be helped," but today was different.

"Why not? She's very worried about you. Why aren't you going home during spring break?"

"Because I don't want to. This is my home now."

"What are you saying? Your mother is waiting. You should at least see her."

Hiroe was about to say, "No," but the dorm mother reached

out before she could respond and grabbed her by the wrist, yanking her up with a fearsome force. Hiroe stumbled out of her room. "Ugh, stop! You're way too strong!"

"You only think so because you're skin and bones. You're as easy to drag along as a toddler."

"Stop it!"

"Listen to me. Talk to your mother."

"No! I said no!"

"Why not?"

Several girls peered out of their rooms, their curiosity roused by the ruckus. Some even came from other floors, wanting to see what the commotion was. Hiroe looked to them for rescue. "Help me, help me!"

Among the onlookers was Mutsumi Tamaki. As Hiroe flung out a fragile arm and tried to touch her, she pulled away and puckered her face. "Ew, don't touch me. How gross." Mutsumi glared coldly at Hiroe with blue eyeshadow-lined eyes under furrowed, thin brows. Hiroe nearly doubted her ears.

Gross? What's so gross about me? I'm not a duck anymore. Who do you think you are calling me gross when I'm way thinner and more stylish than you? You're just jealous!

That's what Hiroe concluded as she looked at Mutsumi's icy profile. Hiroe was four years younger, far prettier and skinnier than she was, so of course she was jealous. *How stupid*, she was about to say as she heard her name fairly screamed out down the corridor. Her mother apparently couldn't wait any longer in the lounge on the first floor and now stood at the bottom of the stairs looking up at Hiroe.

"Hmf," Hiroe snorted. She shook free of the dorm mother's grasp and folded her arms. She clutched her upper arm, the thumb and middle finger of one hand forming a ring around her bicep. She could feel the bones in her arm touching her ribs through her thin skin. *Guys like skinny, slender girls. They want to hug delicate bodies close.*

She knew her real motive was the desire to be attractive to any man. A man far more urbane and refined than that country bumpkin Tatsuro was searching for her. But since she was still in high school they hadn't yet had the opportunity to meet.

"Hiroe! You... You... What happened to you?" Her mother's voice was so choked with tears that it was hard to make out her words. Ever since Hiroe had told her she wasn't going home for spring break, her mother had called nearly every day, eventually coming to Tokyo to get her. Hiroe didn't understand why she was acting that way, even though her mother, the dorm mother and others all said it was because she was worried about her. But Hiroe knew more than anyone else that wasn't the real reason. Her mother was only pretending to be worried. Ever since she was little, her mother only took her outside and bought her all kinds of clothes and toys when it was convenient for her.

"Let's talk, okay? Please tell me whatever is on your mind."

Hiroe was dragged down the stairs and into the lounge and was shocked to see her father standing there. He looked as if he had seen something he wasn't supposed to and reached out for her. Hiroe turned away and ignored her father.

Her mother pressed a kerchief to her mouth and moaned, "You've gotten so thin." Her father restlessly pulled his cigarettes from the breast pocket of his suit.

"Why didn't you notice before it got this bad?" he muttered in a stifled voice.

"Because whenever I asked if she lost weight she just said she was on a diet or had started exercising. She's at the age when girls start worrying about such things, so I figured that was all it was."

"You should have been able to tell that her condition is far more serious than that!"

"Stop shouting!" Hiroe yelled. Both of her parents turned to her with fear in their eyes. "Hmf," she snorted again and crossed her legs under her skirt. Her femurs felt like they clanged together when she laid one across the other. Her calves shivered. "Why are you so worried? Weren't you the ones who were dying to send me to Tokyo? And haven't I kept my grades up just like you told me to?"

"Well, yes, but... But if things were that hard for you, why didn't you tell us sooner?"

"What are you talking about? I told you, it's just a diet."

"But there's a limit. That's what I told you over winter break and you said you understood..." Her mother wept openly and looked at Hiroe with neediness in her eyes. Indeed, when she was home for winter vacation, her mother had tried to get her to go to the hospital, saying that her weight loss was unusual and that she should see a specialist. Hiroe had responded that it wasn't necessary and made a show of eating heaps of food right in front of her. *See? I'm eating.* Besides, Hiroe made sure her mother saw that she looked healthier, livelier and brighter than before. Such displays had made her mother stop voicing her concerns.

"I am eating plenty."

"That doesn't matter if you throw it all back up," her father said, his voice crushed.

Hiroe stared fixedly at her father. "So what?"

"That's unnatural for any person, any living thing to do," he said. But Hiroe had no intention of listening to him. *Food just turns into filthy crap in my stomach. It winds through my intestines and comes out, causing pain and bleeding.* She was still using enemas every day. Even though her bowels were practically water, the pain was still there. Her buttocks were less fleshy than before, but the pain was unchanged. No matter how little she ate, she still had stools.

I don't care if I never have another bowel movement again.

Her father was saying something, but she couldn't parse the words. She let her mind wander. *Is there some way I can plug up my ass?* When her bottom was round, the cheeks were an eyesore. But now that so much of that flesh was gone, instead of having two round cheeks, it simply looked as though there was a broad gap where her thighs met her hips. Hiroe had taken to using the showers recently. It was hard to breathe in the hot baths and soaking in the tub made her pass out.

"Are you listening, Hiroe?"

"Hiroe, please!"

Suddenly she heard voices. She looked anew at her parents as they leaned towards her.

"Let's go to the hospital. You can't stay like this."

"Hospital...?" Hiroe blinked slowly. There was hardly any flesh left along her nose and forehead, to say nothing of her cheeks and eye sockets. Her thin skin looked like it was stretched across her skull. Just pulling her eyelids downwards across her eyeballs and lifting them up again felt like work.

"Okay?"

Her work-loving father and house-hating mother nodded slowly.

"Can they do something for me?"

"What?"

"If they can close up my asshole, then I'll go."

Sew it shut, paste it closed, anything.

"Promise me they'll plug up my anus, and I'll go to the hospital," Hiroe continued, smiling. She saw new dorm residents filing past the window of the lounge.

JAW

1

Black stars flew before Atsushi's eyes. They shot through his dim, warped field of vision, which became streaked with lines of light. Trains rumbled past above his head.

"Know your place!" said a phlegm-coated voice, surprisingly close-by. "You're ten years too young to oppose me. I've never seen such a rotten brat in my life."

Shut up, he wanted to scream, but the punch he'd received was so strong he felt as if there was still a fist in his stomach and he couldn't catch his breath. *Fuck, why does it always have to be like this?*

"Just quit. Go wherever the hell you want." The cheap, hackneyed words continued, ending with a powerful kick to his back. Then the sounds of footsteps moving away. Atsushi placed his cheek against the rough yet cool concrete.

"Are you okay?" came a stranger's voice.

How long has it been? Can I sleep here? he wondered, still laid out, not sure if he was in a dream or reality. *Don't talk to me. Just leave me alone*, he wanted to say, but all he could manage was a quiet groan. As the fogginess in his head began to dissipate, his body throbbed and ached all over. His cheek, stomach, back, legs, elbow... He felt as if his heart had been smashed to bits and scattered throughout his body, and each piece began beating in unison.

"What's wrong? Should I call an ambulance?"

Fuck off. Don't pretend to be kind and take me to the hospital. They'll just call my work, and my boss will tear me a new one and deduct the medical expenses from my already pathetic wages. Since this wasn't Atsushi's first time in such a situation, he knew how it would play out.

"I'm calling one now. Hang in there." Atsushi didn't know who was talking, but the man sounded panicked.

Ugh, whatta pain in the ass.

Atsushi used all his might to push himself up from the concrete. The man was taking his cell phone out of his pocket and staring at Atsushi in surprise. Atsushi had never seen the man before. He wore a suit and necktie, just a run-of-the-mill salaryman.

"Oh, good, you're awake."

Briefly, Atsushi recalled his older brother. The bastard brother who abandoned him and their mother. The brother who always spoke boastfully and left, saying "I'll live how I want to." That brother was doubtlessly now living a neat, compact life in some city, dressed up like a sober businessman. Just because he was a little smarter than average and extremely vain, he treated Atsushi and their mother like they embarrassed him, always talking about "stability" and "normality."

"Are you OK? Here, I'll help."

Atsushi knocked away the salaryman's proffered hand and staggered to a standing position on his own.

"Who did this to you? Some adults are just awful. Did you get in a fight? Did they take your money or something?"

Please, don't talk to me. Don't come near me, or else. I don't know what I'll do to you. Instead of replying, Atsuhi spat bloodied saliva at the man's feet. He staggered away, still gripping his aching abdomen.

"What a way to treat someone who was just trying to help," the man said, predictably spiteful. "Kids shouldn't be loitering around at this time of night. That's why you got into this mess."

You pretend to be helpful, yet this is how you talk to me when I do something you don't like? Atsushi whipped around to face him. The 30-ish salaryman looked momentarily spooked. "Your family must be worried about you," he said, then turned on his heels and walked away.

"Mind your own damn business!" If the man got angry and came back, he'd get beaten up again and end up in an even more wretched state than he was in already. *But that's fine. I want to get beaten to a pulp, lose awareness and disappear completely.*

"Asshole!" Atsushi yelled, as if trying to attack the receding man. At that moment, another train passed by and the narrow walkway beneath the trestle was filled with cacophony. The light from the train windows shone down on the back of the man as he hurried away. The salaryman, slender briefcase in hand, never looked back.

"Shit!" *Everyone is an asshole.* With each shaky step, a sharp pain seared through his solar plexus and the sides of his abdomen. There was no way he could stand up straight as he walked. He'd also apparently suffered a cut somewhere in his mouth, as he could taste something raw and rusty spreading inside. He casually wiped his nose on his arm, and when he pulled it away strands of mostly-dried blood were stuck to it. He was in pretty terrible shape.

Damn Tokyo. This damn city.

Atsushi wondered why he was even there. Half a year gone and he still hadn't found his place, just getting beaten up in filthy places like this.

I hate Tokyo.

But he knew there was nowhere else for him to go. There was no way he could go back home. His mother had her hands full preparing for a life with her new husband, and since she was already caring for his younger siblings he was well aware of what would happen if he went back.

He staggered on through air that clung to his whole body. During summers in the city, it didn't cool off even after the sun set. Gravel and dust still stuck to his sweat-soaked neck.

Where should I go?

If he went back to the decrepit apartment serving as a hostel, that bastard would just say, "Oh, you came back?" and hit him again. "I told you to scram. Or do you want another beating?" He was old but hugely built and beat Atsushi as hard as he could. Just recalling the face of the man he'd spent only three weeks living and working with made him want to stomp on the ground in vexation.

I'm gonna kill you someday. Don't forget it.

Flushed with anger, he repeated the word "kill, kill" over and over in his mind. But eventually it felt pathetic, and an empty, miserable loneliness spread through him. In the gross humidity, he felt a couple of drops of rain fall. He'd thought his only choice was to spend the night in a public park, but if it was raining he truly had nowhere to go. At a loss, he wandered through the night city. He really wanted to go home. He hated Tokyo. But he didn't want to see his new stepfather yell at or hit his mother just for making a sour face. Besides, he didn't even have enough money for train fare.

The rain grew gradually more intense. In an instant, everything around him shone darkly. Atsushi, increasingly resembling a drowned rat, sat underneath the eaves of a shuttered shop. Rain splashed and spattered at his feet.

Money. I need money.

He thought about snatching a purse, or maybe holding up a convenience store. But his stomach and legs still ached. In this state, even if he was able to steal any money, he didn't think he could run away at full speed. He might be able to attack a feeble old lady, but he'd be hard-pressed to find one walking through the rain in the middle of the night.

What should I do. Hell, why was I even born?

He was only 15, but Atsushi began to feel as if there was nothing to look forward to if he kept on living. He felt old age creep-
ing up from the depths of his body. He wouldn't grow any taller.
There was no way for him to become burly or strong.

Suddenly, he recalled Shinjuku. His superior at his old work-
place took him there a while back. He didn't remember where
exactly they had walked, but he found himself on a street corner
that, as night wore on, became crowded with all kinds of men,
Japanese and foreign alike.

"You'd be quite popular, kid. You could make a killing just
spending a little time with these guys," his superior had teased,
only half in jest. Atsushi was short and baby-faced and could
be mistaken for a grade schooler. At those words he'd trembled
in humiliation. As soon as he figured out that his superior, who
had a face like an overripe cucumber, was gay, Atsushi had fled
from that job. What number job was that? How many jobs had he
wandered to and fro since then? But at this point he didn't have
a choice.

I'll try Shinjuku. But will I really be able to get money so easily?

He eagerly lifted up his heavy head and looked up at the
pouring rain. He felt like crying. He wanted to raise his voice and
wail. But Atsushi had forgotten how to cry. He had no intention
of crying, anyways. He stood up and walked out from under the
eaves. Large raindrops furiously struck his entire body, and he
was soaked through in an instant.

Can't I just dissolve in the rain and drain away?

The lump called "Atsushi" would be washed away from the
earth, flowing with the fallen rain into some river, eventually
mixing with dirty water and reaching the sea. Then he'd float
endlessly on the wide open ocean. He'd become consciousness

without a body, maybe someday reaching the shores of his hometown, where his mother was...

"I'm so jealous," came a voice suddenly through the sound of the rain. Atsushi slowly opened his eyes and looked to where the voice was. In the darkness, a disembodied face seemed to float before him. On further inspection, it was a man wearing all black clothing and a close-fitting black hood. Atsushi looked at him, raindrops dripping from his eyelashes.

From the sound of his voice, he was an adult, but rather short, not much taller than Atsushi, who was 5'1". He realized he could steal from a man if he was only this tall. Atsushi was used to brawling which would give him a decent advantage. Even in his current state he knew himself to be plenty nimble. As he'd been staring off into space, the pain in his stomach had lessened considerably. As he flitted from one thought to the next, he drew slowly closer to the man.

"Did you say something?"

The man in the hood was grinning, yet his eyes were as dark as caves and cold enough to send chills up one's spine. *Uh-oh,* thought Atsushi. *I shouldn't get tangled up with someone like this.* The danger signal flickered in his mind. He hadn't done anything, and nothing had happened to him yet, but he wanted to run away. Even so, he was afraid to even break eye contact with the man, so all he could do was stand stock still.

"I'm jealous that you can let the rain soak you." The man's voice was rough, as if coated with sand. Even that terrified Atsushi. He'd sensed a kind of bloodthirst in the coworker who'd just beaten him up, but no matter how badly he was battered he'd never felt fear. Yet this black-garbed man was able to conjure up fear in Atsushi's heart without even lifting a finger.

Atsushi gulped. He tried to step back gingerly, but the man quietly raised his arm and Atsushi froze, unable to move. "Uh...

Y-You can't get wet in the rain?" he asked.

The man stared at him with those cave-like eyes, only his mouth in a smile. "A fight?" he whispered.

"What?"

"Your face."

"Oh," Atsushi said, hurriedly touching his own face. The rain had washed away the grime and dried blood, and the swelling had gone down somewhat. "He was pretty big."

"Someone you don't know?"

"A coworker... My superior at a newspaper distributor." Only a short while ago, Atsushi thought he'd forgotten how to cry, yet now something stirred in his heart. It had been an awfully long time since he'd had the chance to just talk normally with another person.

"Aim for the jaw."

"What?"

As Atsushi stared in puzzlement, the man raised up his arms in a fighting stance and punched the air. His sleeves swooshed as the man's fists danced in the darkness. Atsushi gazed at the hollow-eyed smiling man and felt a thrill run through his biceps.

2

There was dirt in his mouth. It made an awful crunching noise. A sneaker was bearing down on his temple.

"You don't know when to give up, eh, brat?"

He could feel the sneaker's rubber sole on his cheek. He muttered every curse he knew in his mind as he lay prostrate like a worm on the ground.

"I told you whose orders you oughta follow if you wanna stay here. Boy, you sure are stupid."

Just you watch. I'm gonna kill you, Atsushi repeated over and over again in an attempt to forget his present reality.

Why did this always happen to him? Why did this keep happening, no matter how many times he changed jobs?

"If you quit, you've got nowhere else to go, do ya? That's what the boss said. I heard 'im. So you'd better appreciate your superiors. Be more obedient!"

Atsushi didn't know what it meant to be obedient. He'd had similar things yelled at him countless times, yet he never really understood what any of it meant. *"Be modest, you're not nice at all, you're a trickster, you're dishonest, you're nasty, you're too rebellious..." Just fuck off.* That's who he was. It can't be helped. *No one likes me anyways. No one talks to me. That's just who I am.* But he always did exactly as he was told. Atsushi was stupid, so he didn't understand what more he was supposed to do.

"You're cocky just 'cause you're a little cuter than average. But brats like you who leer at women while still wet behind the ears will grow up to be totally useless. Your face sucks, got it?"

He'd never leered intentionally at a woman. Besides, the "woman" the man who was currently crushing Atsushi's face underfoot was referring to was an old hag wearing extremely thick makeup, like a goblin. She'd acted overly friendly, nattering at him as if she were a high-pressure saleswoman. Atsushi only figured out that this man was interested in that goblin when he was called out tonight. Even grasping this fact, Atsushi began to doubt the mental well-being of the man who was stomping on his face. Could he really just humbly listen to what a man who favored monster women had to say?

Sigh. Now I'll have to look for a new job again. More days spent going without food or water, wandering around the city, sneaking about trying to avoid the pigs.

It had only been eight months, yet Atsushi was well aware that he'd have to survive in a world where it would be tough for him to find any job, given that he'd only finished middle school. Apparently the economy was in a recession, and it wasn't rare to see men in their 20's and 30's doing jobs that kids his age would have held in prior years. If he was a little larger, he could work in construction or as a painter, but no matter how many times he applied for such jobs that promised not to inquire about age or academic background, he was always told he was too short. He hated having to call home every time he got a new job, and he was utterly sick of hearing his mother's voice from the receiver asking, "You're fine, aren't you?"

Atsushi vaguely wondered what he should do as he chewed dirt. If he stabbed or killed this man, he wouldn't have to think about where to go—it would be decided for him. Oh, how easy it would be. He wouldn't get the death penalty for such a crime. If he'd be guaranteed a place to live and food to eat, he didn't care which side of the fence he was on. Atsushi felt like he'd be living in a cleaner, more wide-open space that was reasonably safe compared to where he was then.

"It's because shitty little brats like you fall in love with Tokyo that it makes it harder for us guys to live here."

The man put more weight onto his sneaker. Atsushi thought his skull was about to crack. He couldn't cry out, only taste the dirt in his mouth.

"You're a rotten little creep."

His head felt like it would literally split open. If it could, he wished it would. If it did, then this man would become a murderer. If he was a murderer, then he'd have to spend the rest of his life in prison. In any case, either Atsushi or the man would end up living on the other side of the fence.

"Hey!" A voice sounded in the distance. In that moment, the foot bearing down on him quickly relented. This might be his chance. He should knock his leg away, roll over and run away fast. But suddenly there was a thud, and dust floated onto his face. Atsushi opened his eyes in surprise to see the man who'd been attacking him laid out on the ground alongside him. The man was shrieking, covering his face with his hands and writhing about. Atsushi sat up, not sure of what was going on. He looked up and saw a face floating lightly in the darkness. He recognized those cave-like eyes.

"You can't just let 'em keep beating you up." It was the man he'd met in the rain. He was wearing all black clothing and a hood, just like the other time. Atsushi hurriedly stood up. He heard shrieks coming from the ground. Looking down, he saw sticky blood seeping from between the man's fingers as he pressed his hand to his mouth. The man who'd spoken non-stop could now only keen like a kicked dog. Atsushi stared at him in a daze. It had only taken an instant, yet he still couldn't figure out what had happened.

"I saved you. You should say 'thank you,' at least."

"Th-Thank you so much," Atsushi said quickly, bobbing his head. Normally, he'd say something like, "Who asked for your help?" but he instinctively felt that he shouldn't talk back to this man. The hollow-eyed man, smiling only with his lips, nodded and said, "Good. Now call an ambulance. He won't die, but he'll be in the hospital for a while."

"Really?" Atsushi said, his eyes wide. The man pointed to something. Atsushi turned to look and saw the light of a public phone booth.

"Call 911 from there. If you don't want to get in trouble for this, then just go on back home afterwards."

I see, thought Atsushi as he started off towards the phone booth. A thought came to him and he stopped in his tracks. "But he might talk. He'll say it was your fault."

The black-garbed man smiled in satisfaction and moved his face close to the crumpled man on the ground. "This is your punishment for picking on the weak. Now your body knows what'll happen if you do it again." The man was curled up in a ball, blood spewing voluminously from his mouth. Yet even in this unsightly state he frantically nodded his head. Once the man confirmed this, he straightened himself, told Atsushi to hurry up and make the call, then scurried away. Atsushi watched him melt into the darkness, still half in a stupor.

Wow. He figured the man must have been a boxer. But he didn't see what move he used or how fast he'd taken down Atsushi's superior. He regretted that terribly.

3

His coworker had a broken jaw. It would take a full three months to heal. Yet he said he remembered nothing about his attacker. He said he'd been walking through the city at night when suddenly someone punched him. The manager told all the employees that although the man was a hard worker he was only part-time, so he asked him to quit. For the first time in his life, Atsushi was able to relish the feeling that he'd survived.

"The economy being what it is I can't just hire more guys, so we'll have to make do with the people we've got left. I'm counting on you, too, Atsushi. Maybe someday you'll even work in the kitchen." Atsushi was surprised at how happy the boss's words made him.

This means I can stay. He'd never thought that not being forced to wander aimlessly through the city would make him feel so relieved.

For the time being, while no one was openly hostile towards Atsushi, his days were still far from pleasant. Especially in the evenings, as he watched boys and girls around his age dressed in school uniforms loitering about all carefree, he became exceedingly angry. He knew that he needed to avoid making waves and continue working at his current job for as long as possible. But three days passed, then a week, and a gloomy sensation bubbled up like gas throughout his body and he grew irritable. He wanted to lash out at every little thing said by his bosses, superiors or even the older lady who worked part-time. It wasn't that he couldn't hold down a job. But once he felt he'd gotten the hang of whatever was required of him, he'd felt this same sort of vexation well up and he'd clash unnecessarily with someone or show insubordination. Countless times he was told he didn't know his place, he'd tempt someone into hurting him. He didn't know why, but he wanted to rage. Even though he knew he'd lose, he just wanted to explode his gloominess in someone's face.

Atsushi managed to hold down his job for an entire month. Payday came. He wanted to go out into the city that night. Not that he had anything in particular he wanted to do. As he strolled along, he became increasingly agitatedt. All the people going past him seemed so happy. The girls in their school uniforms playing around until late at night lived with their parents, never knowing hardship. They seemed to exist in a separate universe.

He bought cigarettes from a vending machine. *Might as well get drunk*, he thought as he glared at everybody who passed him as he walked. If anyone even dared to make eye contact with him he'd use that as an excuse to pick a fight. That was the kind of mood he was in. Yet happy or unhappy, everyone walked on by without looking at him, as if they didn't even notice that he existed.

What the hell. Dammit! They're all making fun of me! Now I wanna rumble with someone. A drunkard would be good. If I see someone who looks weak and staggers along, I'll punch him as hard as I can. The irritation inside of him now crystallized into hatred that swelled to the point of bursting.

He ducked into a less-trafficked street and observed the gaits of people coming from the train station. Atsushi slowed his own steps. A man was walking towards him, alone. He was in his 40's and hustling along in a busy manner.

No.

Next, a woman. *No.* Third up, an old man. *No, no, no, no.* His infuriation ballooned. If he didn't hit someone, anyone, his rage would become uncontrollable. Atsushi walked back and forth down the street, earnestly searching for a target. The night wind had grown chilly, and crickets chirped weakly from between the crowded houses.

What am I doing, he suddenly wondered. *Wandering around just to find someone I don't even know and punch them? I must really be stupid.* Stupid. That's what his older brother who'd abandoned them had often lamented. *You're so stupid. If you don't get it together you're gonna end up in a world of hurt*, he'd told Atsushi who was just a grade schooler at the time. *The only cure for stupidity is death.*

Fuck, why'd I have to remember something like that? He didn't even care if he couldn't find a human target. He wanted to throw rocks at someone's windows or set fire to piles of garbage, anything to help him let off some steam. With this new goal in mind, Atsushi started walking again. At that moment he caught sight of a figure tottering along. Atsushi's heart leaped. He unconsciously balled up his hands into fists inside his jeans' pockets.

The figure seemed to be either sick or drunk. He walked very slowly on a diagonal path down the street. His head swung back and forth and even from a distance he looked to be so drained of energy that it was a miracle he was able to stand up or walk at all.

Atsushi was used to seeing drunks. His mother worked at a small bar before she remarried. Atsushi would lead his hungry little brother and sister to the bar. "Hurry up and eat before the Madam sees you," their mother would say as she handed them hastily-made rice balls at the back entrance. Sometimes he'd have to wait for her until the bar closed, his fussing sister strapped to his back. He'd wait, wanting to tell her what he needed to bring to school the next day, even knowing he'd get scolded. On each of those occasions, Atsushi saw drunken men. They'd laugh with loud, vulgar voices, grab his mother's ass, tell filthy jokes.

Bingo.

There's no way he'd lose to an opponent like that. Besides, such a man wouldn't even remember getting beat up the next day. Atsushi felt his tension heighten as he closed in on the man.

The streetlights lit up the drunk. He was in a suit, minus a tie. His hair was a mess, but he was unexpectedly young. He leaned against a lamppost. He looked ill, his back arched forward and his head hanging.

If he vomits it'll be hard to hit him.

Atsushi crept closer to the man, careful not to alert him to his presence. Suddenly he heard loud sniffling. Beneath the dim streetlight, he could see something dripping from the man's face.

He was crying. A sob escaped his mouth as tears and snot streamed from his face as he wept, beating his fist against the lamppost. Half dumbfounded, Atsushi watched this pitiable display from a distance.

"Don't hit someone like him," a voice suddenly came from behind him. Startled, Atsushi whipped around and saw the black-garbed man, again wearing a fitted hood, looking at him with those hollow eyes. "You had your eye on him, didn't you?"

"Uh... No..."

"Don't act like such a coward. Aim for someone stronger than yourself." The man smacked Atsushi on the shoulder and darted away. Atsushi stared idly at the man as he occasionally stopped to jab at the darkness, dashing away nimbly leaving behind only the sound of swishing fabric. Atsushi hurried after him, but the man was surprisingly fast on his feet. As soon as he turned a corner, he lost him completely. Atsushi stood alone on a deserted street trying to catch his breath. The full-to-bursting irritation he'd felt had been squashed flat, and in its place an odd sense of defeat spread through his chest.

Someone stronger than myself.

Atsushi had been aiming for someone stronger until recently. He'd taken on bigger men more used to fighting and had always ended up in a sorry state. He felt pathetic once he realized that at some point he'd started targeting men who were weaker than himself.

I wanna become strong enough to take on men bigger than me and win.

The next day, he found boxing magazines in a convenience store. He bought several without bothering to check them out beforehand. He read them intently, cover to cover, over and over again. At night he'd wander around his neighborhood. He wanted to see the black-garbed man again. He wanted to become his disciple, to learn boxing at the same gym he did. This was the first hope he'd had since moving to Tokyo.

The second payday came and went. Atsushi bought more boxing magazines and approached his boss with a question.

"You wanna join a gym?"

Atsushi could feel himself blushing up to his ears. "Yes," he nodded. He didn't really understand why he was so embarrassed. But it sounded like an admission of weakness, and it made him feel very uncomfortable. His boss might scorn him, laugh at him, tease him. Atsushi had worried over it all month long, finally concluding that he wanted to become stronger, even if it cost him his job. No matter how much he searched he still hadn't found the black-garbed man. But sitting around waiting for a chance encounter wouldn't make him the least bit stronger. His only choice was to work out by himself.

"You're free to do as you please so long as it doesn't interfere with work. Why not do something you like?" his boss replied, unexpectedly easily. Atsushi felt like he'd dodged a blow. "This isn't a school. You can do whatever you want with your pay as long as you work hard."

His boss's words were blunt, yet Atsushi was so happy that his chest grew hot. He realized that working and receiving pay for a whole two months was practically a first for him. Until now, he'd asked for whatever he was owed partway through the month so he could run away, which always pissed off his bosses. Sometimes he'd even worked without compensation for just a few days before sneaking away.

"If I was in your shoes I'd consider going to night school, but if you wanna learn how to box I've got no reason to say no. As long as you can take care of your own business, I can't complain." The boss, busy as usual, slapped him on the shoulder with finality and walked away. Atsushi sighed with relief and felt his chest swell with a new sensation. He could already see himself in the ring, unleashing blows with his bright red gloves.

Atsushi chose a gym out of the countless places that advertised in the back of the boxing magazines. All the ads were filled with all kinds of enticing phrases: "Accepting New Students!" "Beginners Welcome!" "Housing Available!" More than a few gyms were run by well-known boxers. There were tons of gyms within city limits. Once he realized how many people there were who wanted to learn boxing and get stronger, he felt he couldn't be so lazy anymore.

The man in black might have been inspired to learn boxing after reading magazines, too. *Maybe he was weak like me, getting beat up all the time,* he thought, letting his imagination run wild. He chose a gym in his neighborhood. He didn't know whether it was nice or shoddy, top-flight or third-rate. He simply chose it because it was the closest one advertised.

"Any experience?" asked the president of the gym when Atsushi went to observe a class.

"No," he answered, his face flushed red. The ad said beginners were welcome, so he didn't think he'd be turned away. Yet he was on tenterhooks, expecting the president to tell him to give up.

"Hunh. So you're a total newbie, eh?" the president asked in a thick, husky voice. He was older and heavy set. He looked more like a former wrestler than a boxer. Atsushi simply nodded.

"Any good at fighting?"

"No."

"Ever get beaten up?"

"More times than I can count." Atsushi wanted to be as honest as possible, figuring there was no point in acting tough.

"A weakling?" the president laughed in a voice so loud Atsushi felt his eardrums reverberate. "So you wanna get strong?"

"I do." Atsushi felt like crying. *Yes. I want to be strong. I wanna be stronger than everyone else.*

"How old are you?"

"I turned 16 last week." He'd spent his birthday all alone. He'd expected at least his mother to call, but she never did. There was no one on earth who even remembered his birthday, let alone wanted to celebrate it with him.

"Well, wanna go see a class? You can decide after that," the president said. Atushi nodded faintly.

It was his first time inside a boxing gym and it was a mysterious place indeed. There were at least a dozen men, yet not a single voice could be heard. The only sounds were inorganic, emanating from the equipment as the men jumped rope, did warm-ups or punched sandbags suspended from the ceiling.

The whole place smelled unfamiliar. Nearly half the space was taken up by the ring, upon which a man shadow boxed. Another man stood on the other side, punching mitts worn by his partner. Each man moved silently as if every other person in the place was invisible. A bell rang, signaling the end of the three-minute workout period and everyone stopped what they were doing and moved on to the next exercise area or took a drink of water. Another bell rang a minute later and everyone started working out again.

Three minutes passed. The bell rang. People moved. A minute passed. The men started working again as if tiredness was a foreign concept. Atsushi watched, never losing interest, as men in their 40's and 50's entered, followed by girls around 20 years old. They changed into gym clothes and joined the silent three-minute-one-minute pattern of movement.

The alloted time for observation had passed. "There's a 'health and beauty' course targeted for women, and a 'stress relief' course for businessmen. Five courses in all. Which one do you wanna try?" the president asked, handing Atsushi a blue guidebook.

He looked at each of the offerings and stated without hesitation, "The professional training course." The president, who resembled a *daruma* doll, pulled his chin back in surprise.

"You gotta be kidding. The rules, the training regimen, everything will be much tougher than the other courses. You'll have to come here every single day."

"I want to be a pro."

"You wanna go pro, eh? Hmm." The president straightened up slightly and looked at Atsushi with new eyes. In boxing, one's class is determined by one's body weight. No matter how small or weak Atsushi seemed, there must be a class that he belonged to. Yet even though the roly-poly president stared at him with narrowed eyes, he no longer blushed. All he wanted was to climb into the ring and punch something as hard as he could.

"Then dye your hair back to black and cut it short."

"My hair?"

"We ask everyone who says they want to go pro to prove their readiness by changing their hair."

Atsushi's hair was long, nearly brushing his shoulders. He was told at each new job that he had to cut it, but he'd never listened. He also dyed it himself, which caused others to tease him, saying he looked like a girl.

"I'll do it by tomorrow," Atsushi said, puffing his chest out.

The president grinned for the first time and placed a hand on Atsushi's head. "See ya tomorrow, then." Atsushi felt the warmth from the man's large palm through his hair. He suddenly felt like he'd returned to childhood and answered, "Yes," as the president rocked his head.

4

The next day, Atsushi's life changed completely. He quit smoking the cigarettes he'd gotten used to. He stopped drinking even the occasional beer. Just those changes gave him a bit more leeway with his monthly budget. What he spent on cigarettes and alcohol he now used entirely for boxing. Gym clothes, towels, t-shirts and the like he could buy at cheap stores but proper shoes and gloves were surprisingly expensive. He didn't even have money left over to go to the arcades anymore. Everything in his life revolved around boxing.

The first several weeks were spent in basic training. He learned proper stretching, how to skip rope and lift weights.

"If you can't do the basic training, then you won't be able to do the rest of the training, either. Don't worry about doing anything else, just do whatever I tell you to do and do it well." The president said the same thing to all the trainees. Atsushi focused on learning the order of stretches and skipping rope until it went smoothly and spent all his time building up strength, especially in the muscles in his neck. The only boxing-like things he learned were the basic stances, footwork and how to throw a straight left punch. Even so, he never felt bored. Work for three minutes. Rest for one minute. Work again. This repetition was more enjoyable than anything else in his life.

The men who worked out at the gym were of various ages and had all kinds of occupations. They were instructed to greet one another politely, but aside from that hardly anyone made small talk. Everyone was focused strictly on their own forms, silently striving towards their own goals. Simply being among them allowed Atsushi to forget his loneliness, his irritation, his hatred and anger towards random people. The more he sweat and the harder he worked his body, the quieter his mind became. That quiet was comfortable.

On days he worked the early shift, he left in the evening and went straight to the gym. On days he worked the late shift, he worked out early in the morning. Recently his muscles were sore all over and his body was tired, leaving him sleepy at work, but in order to keep boxing he needed to secure a steady income. He worked hard and kept his head down. When he had free time he went running. He added push-ups and sit-ups to his routine at home. He never thought about anything besides training.

At long last he was taught the straight right, footwork and the 1-2-3 combination. Atsushi realized he was a bit stronger than when he hadn't done any training at all.

Out of the blue, his mother called one night towards the end of the year. "Don't you get a break for New Year's? When are you coming home?"

"I'm not."

"What? But you didn't even come home for *o-bon*."

"I'm busy."

"Oh, really? You still working at the same job?"

"Yes, that's why I'm here," he said in a stifled voice.

"Okay, well, take care of yourself," his mother said, sounding lonesome. "I'm worried about you."

"Don't be." Atsushi should have been happy to hear from his mother, but he felt that old irritation for being pulled back to reality. He had to bite back the words: *As if I can go back to that house. Where the hell am I supposed to sleep?* Atsushi no longer wanted to think about anything that would distract him from boxing.

Atsushi had planned on spending his first New Year's in Tokyo alone with a bento box from a convenience store, but he was pleasantly surprised when the president of the gym invited him over to his house.

"Boxers have to have a strictly balanced diet. Plus, you're in a growth spurt. You gotta eat good, nutritious food."

Atsushi was grateful. He felt like he'd finally found someone in Tokyo that he could honestly say "thank you" to. He could trust what this man said. He felt that as long as he followed his instructions, he could become a proper boxer, and that made him happy.

Next he learned shadow boxing and how to punch mitts. Once a week he was allowed to spar, then learn defensive moves, and found himself completely absorbed in real boxing. His muscles grew stronger and his footwork lighter. He could circle and thought he was pretty good at dodging blows. He wanted to test his strength outside. He thought that if he encountered the men who had beaten him up, there was no way he'd just take it lying down like he had before. In fact, he'd probably be able to unleash several punches on them first.

"Listen, don't get mixed up in brawls outside. You're gonna be a professional. Your fists aren't just any fists. Amateurs will see them as dangerous weapons," the president pressed, as if he could see right into Atsushi's mind. He had decided to obey this man, so although he was disappointed, he nodded meekly. Boxing is a sport. He wouldn't get into fights anymore. Instead he would focus all the anger, resentment and hatred that had grown inside him since birth into his fists whenever he was in the ring. That was all he wished for.

With each turn of the seasons, Atsushi made more progress and grew slightly taller. When he first started training, he'd expected to be in the lowest weight division, or possibly light flyweight, but surprisingly, when he was getting closer to qualifying as a pro, he was 122 pounds. He'd practiced self-restraint and avoided fatty foods, and if he worked at losing weight, the lightest he'd get would be about 110 pounds. Flyweight was the division that best suited him.

Atsushi never quarreled with anyone at work, and nobody messed with him in return. Everyone knew his name, and while they called him a "boxing maniac" behind his back, no one said anything nasty to his face. Since he was able to push his body to the limit everyday, he rarely felt irritated. In fact, he maintained an inner tranquility he'd never experienced before. The nights he spent wandering the city looking for weak prey felt like a distant memory.

One day he'd stand in the ring at Korakuen Hall. He'd wear a boxing gown and walk towards the dazzlingly bright ring as fans cheered him from the stands. That was his only dream.

Aside from New Year's vacation, he never skipped a day at the gym. He went running any chance he could get and the next year he turned 17, took the long-awaited professional test and passed with flying colors.

"Well, if you couldn't pass the test then you should quit," said the president, cooly. "All that's left is to see how many fights you can get through."

Indeed, he knew from talking to older boxers at the gym and reading magazines that just passing the test didn't mean he'd be accepted as a professional boxer. Win or lose, he needed to compete. He needed to build experience in the ring.

"Will you set up matches for me?"

"Calm your horses. We need to find you a suitable fight partner for your debut match."

Atsushi was nonplussed by the president's indifferent response. Any and all fights had to be set up under the direction of the president. No matter how badly Atsushi wanted to fight, he couldn't do anything on his own.

"You should focus on keeping yourself in fighting form so you can take on any opponent at any time. If you wanna earn money boxing, training is still the most important thing. I'll take care of all the annoying business, so you should just keep getting stronger."

Atsushi trained all the time, even harder than before. Although he was technically a pro, little had changed—he still spent every day shuttling between the gym and work. The only difference was that his photo now hung in the "Pro Boxers of this Establishment" corner of his gym.

5

In his debut match, Atsushi knocked out his opponent in the 2nd round. Tension caused his mind to go blank and he didn't quite know what he was doing, but he threw a left hook on the spur of the moment and his opponent's jaw seemed to distort from the impact. The man had an oval face like an inverted triangle. He went down to the mat, knocked out with a concussion. The next thing Atsushi knew, the referee was pulling up his hand as the crowd burst into applause.

"Guys with long jaws like that aren't cut out for boxing. Like the pendulum theory, a punch that lands on a distended jaw will rock the whole skull," explained the president, smiling happily for the first time.

In boxing, injuries to the head and body are different. While body blows are painful and can cause lasting damage, a hit to the bead can twist the brain stem, the brain can rotate backwards within a shaken skull, and reverberations can cause instantaneous concussions. So even if a boxer can withstand punches to the body, there's no way of enduring or fighting through a punch to the face. Plus, bulking up muscles helps train the body for impact, but with the head, the most one can do is to build up muscles along the neck. Even if the blow is softened, there's only so much that can lessen a direct impact to the brain which sits like a block of tofu in water.

"Everything helps you gain experience, but you need to avoid getting hit like that. It'll help you stay alive, let alone keep competing in the ring. You gotta get better at defensive moves."

So that's why. It's not like getting hit by an amateur. No matter how much I train, I don't wanna get nailed in the face by a pro boxer's glove. In order to get stronger, he wasn't allowed to neglect defense training. He learned something new with each match, throwing himself into practice.

He also endured the pain of having to lose weight before fights. He was able to keep his hunger in check for a week. His body seemed totally clear and he felt like he'd avoided being careless, yet at night he'd dream of eating, and he'd wake cursing himself and he'd vomit reflexively.

Harder still was limiting his water intake. If he needed to lose weight even after spending day after day training without eating at all, he'd also have to stop drinking water. His tongue would dry out and he'd even stop sweating. At such times, if he took a bath his skin would suck up the bathwater. He couldn't let rain touch him. He wore a sauna suit when he went running at dawn and dusk in order to force his body to sweat and to keep dry in case of a sudden downpour.

The first time he had to focus on losing weight he learned just how hard it was to work in the food industry. He'd acted tough, saying he needed to work in a restaurant in order to cultivate the mental fortitude necessary to resist temptation, but he only lasted until the time came for his second diet, as it was just too difficult to be surrounded by delicious-looking food and drink at work.

Ever since Atsushi told his manager at work that he wanted to join a gym, he'd been very sympathetic to his desires, even arranging his work schedule to accommodate him. "Thanks for working so hard for us for such a long time. Hurry up and become a champion. We'll go watch your fights," the manager said. Everyone at work saw him off on his final day. "I'll do my best," he said, and left. That was the first time he'd been able to take leave of a job in such a manner. Until now his bosses would berate him and he'd have to flee without even saying goodbye to the coworkers he'd gotten friendly with and have to find a new job fast. It was the first time in a while that something had happened in his daily life that made his heart burn hotly.

His new day job was working for a small printing office. The CEO was a longtime friend of the gym president and knew all about boxing. He welcomed Atsushi, who at that point had already passed his qualifying test.

"We don't pay very much, but you should feel comfortable working here. Anyways, you should focus on making money with those boxing gloves instead," the CEO said at their first meeting. He no longer felt irritated with his superiors even when he was the new kid at work. There were less than a dozen employees, over half of which were in their 40's and 50's. Since everyone already knew Atsushi was a boxer, no one gave him any guff.

The printing office reeked of paper and ink. The work was simple, and while his job required a fair amount of brute strength, for the times he had to go without eating he was thankful to pass the days quietly in a place that had such a terrible smell. Atsushi worked even harder training for boxing.

Matches were arranged. Training was scheduled. Days spent in preparation for just one event. Diets endured. Matches fought. When he won, he felt relieved and could eat as much of his favorite foods as he wanted, but when he lost, depending on how badly he was injured, he might not have any appetite at all and would wallow in self-pity instead. He spent his days shuttling between the printer and the gym, running as fast as he could. At first he was doing 4-round fights, then he moved up to 6-rounds, then graduated to the top level of licensed boxers. He turned twenty years old.

Once in a while, his mother would call. "Are you really gonna keep doing such a dangerous sport? Are you really okay?" She'd complain about her new husband for a while and tell him how his younger siblings were faring, then worry aloud about his chosen sport, saying over and over how scary it was. "Can't you find something else to do? You don't have to keep doing something so scary."

"There's nothing else I can do."

"That's just an excuse. You could get a driver's license, work as a cabbie. It's important to learn some real skills. Please? Give up boxing, it's too scary."

He hadn't seen his mother in years, yet hearing her voice did nothing except irritate him. *I box because its dangerous. I chose it because I wanted a way to vent all my anger.* But telling her as much wouldn't convince her. He wanted to climb into the four-cornered ring and punch his opponent as hard as he could. If he could continue living that dream, he had no need for women or alcohol.

"That's pretty rare nowadays. That used to be a superstition in the past, but I don't care at all if you have a girlfriend," the president would say on occasion, sounding mystified. Atsushi would only smile vaguely in response then go back to training alone. When he would shadow box, he'd use the large mirror that hung on the wall. He noticed that he'd lost his babyface, and in fact looked a bit older than his years. His well-trained body was covered with taught muscles from his neck down to his calves and was devoid of any trace of extraneous fat. Atsushi trusted and loved his body, more than anything else in the world, the body that looked so different under the uniform he wore at work.

However, his track record was far from stellar. Although he'd won his debut match with a KO, afterwards he won some matches and lost others. His path in the boxing world wasn't as smooth as he'd hoped.

I wanna climb the rankings, at least get into the top ten in Japan. That was Atsushi's only dream. He fought in four or five matches a year and spent the rest of his time training tirelessly. Atsushi's days were extremely quiet.

The accident happened two years later. As a fully-grown adult, Atsushi was barely still eligible to fight in the flyweight division, but that's where he wanted to remain. If he moved up to super flyweight he knew he wouldn't have to fret over diets anymore, but there was a boxer in his division that he was determined to defeat.

He continued his severe dieting, just barely clearing the weight limit. But during the match that day his body felt sluggish and his legs were very heavy.

This is weird. Something's wrong.

But it was too late. He only realized that his body's condition was abnormal right after the starting bell sounded. His body didn't move the way he wanted it to. Normally his muscles would move before he even thought about it, but now he felt clumsy and stiff.

Atsushi measured the distance between himself and his opponent as they began exchanging light jabs. Then his opponent threw a straight punch right towards his face. In that instant all his practice and his flawless image training should have kicked in, but instead his heart was gripped with terror.

Oh, no. What's wrong? It's never like this, he panicked. His punches were lifeless and only occasionally connected, so his opponent was in fine form. *He's reading me, able to sense every move I make.* This realization made him even more scared. The ring became an inescapable execution site.

"What's wrong with you? You're not acting like yourself. Calm down, circle left. Circle, keep circling closer!" his trainer shouted fiercely once the bell rang and he retired to his corner. Atsushi nodded, but the words didn't reach his ears.

I wanna run away, get away from the ring. But the bell rang again. His opponent was younger and lower ranked than Atsushi but rumor had it that he could compete at the international level someday. The young man's body glistened with sweat as he hopped around happily before Atsushi.

Just one punch.

After repeatedly getting forced into the corner constantly on the defense, this was his conclusion. He'd suffered countless blows since the first round and his vision was wobbly. His legs, heavy to begin with, now felt like lead. He didn't want to drag out this match any longer. He had to aim for his opponent's face, even though it might be impossible. The jaw. Aim for the jaw.

But his own commands, let alone those of his trainer, felt fuzzy and unreliable, as if they came from a distance through a dense fog. His trainer was yelling something. The roar of the crowd surrounded him like waves. The light bearing down on the right was as bright as a midsummer sun. The only sounds he could hear were his own breathing and the blows from his opponent's gloves landing on his supposedly well-trained body. He'd been hit countless times in the liver. His body twisted in pain.

Eighth round. He had no idea what he was doing anymore. Then came the president's voice through the din: "Calmly, calmly! Move in on him, Atsushi!" He snapped back to his senses. He watched as his opponent threw a punch that looked bizarrely slow.

Shit. I won't be able to dodge this one.

The right hook connected with his temple. Atsushi heard a noise like that of dry wood snapping. The light shining down from above went black.

I was lonely. Always so lonely.

He thought he could hear voices. He was neither hot nor cold and his body was free of pain. He slowly opened his eyes. A train roared past. A child lay sprawled out beneath the darkened trestle.

Help me. I'm scared. I'm lonely.

The voice seemed to be coming from the boy. Atsushi gazed at him. He suddenly wondered why he was there, but he couldn't remember. This place wasn't anywhere near his usual running course, yet it felt strangely familiar.

"Are you okay?" A salaryman approached the boy, but the boy got up, sulking, and knocked the man's hand away.

"Mind your own damn business!" the boy yelled in a hoarse voice. But what Atsushi heard was: "Don't go. Stay with me. Why does everyone leave me?" The boy's heart was breaking. The boy trudged away. Atsushi followed him, feeling like he'd seen him somewhere. The boy looked terribly lonesome, as if he were crying with his whole body as he walked through the dingy streets.

I have nowhere to go. I wanna go home, his back seemed to mutter as raindrops began to fall.

Oh, no. I gotta lose weight. The rain is my enemy. Atsushi took cover from the rain under the eaves of a store and gazed at the boy. *Looks like he needs money. If he can't steal any, he might become a male prostitute.*

"I'm so jealous," he said without thinking. The boy looked at him through the rain with eyes that gleamed like black flames. He was lonely and wanted to cry, yet his eyes showed that all he knew was how to hate people.

"A fight?"

"What?"

"Your face."

"Oh. He was pretty big."

"Someone you don't know?"

"A coworker... My superior at a newspaper distributor."

"Aim for the jaw." That's right. One blow to the jaw. You can't protect the jaw. Even if you can't break it, you can still do a ton of damage to the brain.

"Please, doctor, help him!" came the president's voice from

afar. Atsushi turned away from the boy and leant an ear to the voice.

"I've done all I can. But there's nothing I can do to bring him back to consciousness," said a voice he didn't recognize. The president was yelling his name. "Come on, Atsushi. Wake up! Please!"

What is he talking about? Where am I, anyway? I can't just sit here wasting time. I gotta aim for the jaw, the jaw, the jaw.

He wandered through a world shrouded in heavy mist. Suddenly he came across the boy he'd seen earlier. He was on the ground, getting beaten up again, kicked in the stomach and the face.

Help. Help! the boy's heart screamed. *Sheesh, why doesn't he just ask for help? Why doesn't he fight back?* thought Atsushi. The president had warned him against fighting outside, but he had to make an exception. Atsushi crept up close to the man who was stomping on the boy and threw a light uppercut at his jaw. He heard an odd, dry cracking noise. The noise reverberated throughout his entire body and head, never fading away.